A Kahale and Claude Mystery Series

Book 1:

CAMP

LENAPE

Timothy R. Baldwin

D1488047

Indies United Publishing House, LLC

ISBN-13: 978-1-64456-076-1

Library of Congress Control Number: 2019952982

www.indiesunited.net

For my students, past and present.

Prologue

Deep in the Allegheny Mountains, three young men stood on a narrow, dirt road. It was dark save for a battery-powered lantern that sat before the men as if holding a conference with them. The lantern's glow gave off just enough illumination that the men could see their own breath as they exhaled into the chilly, late winter night.

Erik Novak's neatly trimmed beard and trendy, East Coast clothing set him apart as the leader of the trio. He glared at the two younger men, Paul and Joey Meier, who stood on either side of him. They were brothers, a few years apart, with patchy beards, dressed in faded flannels. Paul was a few years older than Joey. Where Paul was short and broad, Joey was tall and scrawny.

They were inexperienced, but Erik had limited time and needed the help of the locals. Checking his watch, Erik huffed. Paul, the older of the two brothers, had promised a contact, Uncle Tommie, who was supposed to show five minutes ago. Erik opened his mouth to speak to the brothers and send them away, but the sound of crunching leaves from the thicket of brush and pine behind the men caused him to turn in expectation.

Uncle Tommie, a neatly dressed man in his sixties, appeared. Though Erik couldn't make out every detail of the man's features, he immediately recognized the toothy, mustached grin from the pictures Paul had shown him.

"See, boss," said Paul as he bounced on his tiptoes. "I told you Uncle Tommie would show."

"You did," Erik said through clenched teeth. He turned to Uncle Tommie. "Nice to do business with you, Uncle—"

"Just Tom," said the older man, cutting off Erik. "It's nice doing business with you as well."

Erik extended his hand, and Tom shook it. The older man's grip was firm. As the two men released their handshake, Erik noticed a twitch in Tom's eye and looked at him coldly.

"You're late," Erik said.

Tom didn't reply. He didn't need to. The four of them were suddenly awash with the light of an approaching sedan.

"No, I'm not late," said Tom. He pointed at the car. "They are."

When the car stopped ten feet in front of the men, the doors opened. Two men, one in his thirties with a full head of jet-black hair and the other of an ambiguous older age with a clean-shaven head, got out. The older, bald man approached the group while the younger man remained near the car with his hand resting on a gun holstered at his hip.

"Erik," Tom said. "I want you to meet…"

"Dick, or you can call me Richard," said the older man, extending his hand to Erik, who took it. "I understand we are to use first names."

"You're correct," Erik said. "It's better that way." Erik glanced behind Richard. "Who's the other guy?"

"That's Neil. He doesn't talk much." Richard rubbed a hand over his bald head.

Erik scratched his bearded cheek and glanced at Tom. Other than the twitch in his right eye, Tom stood there completely relaxed.

"You two are good with the arrangement?" asked Erik.

"We are," Richard said as he turned to Tom. "But this is a big ask."

Tom blinked. "Dick, you know how important this is."

"I do," Richard said. "You don't need to remind

me. Besides, I've got retirement to look forward to, and this is going to help a lot."

"Yes, it will," Tom said. He cleared his throat as he glanced at Erik.

"Excellent," said Erik. "Shall we proceed?"

The two older men nodded to each other.

"Go ahead," Tom said.

Erik held out an open palm to Paul, one of his scruffy sidekicks, who produced two thick envelopes.

"This should be sufficient for the next few months," Erik said as he handed an envelope to Tom and the other to Richard. "You know what's expected."

"We do," the two older men said simultaneously as if rehearsed.

"You both understand that Detroit won't be happy if they're double-crossed," Erik said sternly.

Both older men shifted their weight. Even Neil stood erect next to the car where he'd been casually leaning.

"Excellent," Erik said. "We'll revisit in, say, three months."

The two older men each shook hands with Erik. They stuffed their envelopes into their pockets, sealing an unwritten contract agreed upon months ago. Tom turned and disappeared into the darkness of the forest. Richard returned to the sedan where Neil was already seated in the passenger seat. Richard slammed the door shut and backed the vehicle up, leaving the other men to squint and shield their eyes from the glare of the headlights.

When the sedan was gone and the glow of the lantern was all that illuminated the trio, Paul broke the silence.

"You sure you can trust them?" Paul asked.

"You sure I can trust you two?" asked Erik as he glared at the scruffy brothers. They were hired hands, but more importantly, they were clean.

"You can count on it, boss," Joey chimed in, far too eager to impress the boss.

Paul slapped his younger brother in the back of the head. Joey rubbed his head but didn't whine about being hit.

"Good," Erik said. "Joey, grab the lantern. We've got work to do."

Without waiting for a response, Erik entered the shadows of the forest, stopping momentarily for the lantern's glow to catch up with him. Erik preferred to do business with people he knew, but time was of the essence. Besides, these two men, just like the three that had left, were dispensable, and he would not hesitate to act against them, should the need arise.

PART ONE

Chapter 1

Monday, July 16.

Under the blue skies overlooking Camp Lenape on a sunny afternoon, Marcus Kahale stood as the third-base coach. He pulled his hair back and off his neck, in anticipation of the afternoon's heat. At first base, Alissa Claude took her position as coach. She doused water over her long braids, then shook out the excess. Marcus grinned until Alissa realized he was watching her. She waved at him.

"Get ready!" Alissa shouted.

Marcus flashed her an exaggerated thumbs-up. He had a sparkle in his hazel eyes. Marcus and Alissa, like the other teens taking their places in the outfield, were junior camp counselors. Both had aged out of Camp Lenape's summer program after completing their freshman year of high school the previous year. They, like their peers, had been exemplary campers. Mr. Roberts, the camp director, taking up a position on the pitcher's mound, had offered them the opportunity to work at camp.

Mr. Roberts had grown up at the camp, a baseball camp founded by his father sixty years ago. He'd gone on to pitch in the minor leagues in his twenties, but an injury brought him back to the camp a few years later. Some thirty years ago, Mr. Roberts had inherited the camp when his father passed away. He made the progressive decision to expand the program to include girls. Baseball was now just one of the outlets Mr. Roberts used to teach the core camp principles of personal character, leadership, and teamwork.

"All right, campers," said Mr. Roberts. His voice sounded a little nasally, as it always did when he was excited and had to project his voice to a large audience. "As most of you know, today marks the first of our house games. Let's hear it for your junior counselors." Mr. Roberts paused dramatically as a hundred and twenty campers, plus their senior counselors, cheered.

Mr. Roberts rattled off a bunch of names, with each junior counselor striking some pose or doing some dance that drove the kids wild. This included Janice and Nate, who were best friends to Alissa and Marcus. They, like the other junior camp counselors, were assigned to specific cabin groups for the summer. When the final names were announced, and the cheers came to a crescendo, Mr. Roberts, like an orchestra conductor, raised his hands and silenced the voices of every camper.

"Alrighty, kids," Mr. Roberts said. "Up today, we have the Blue Dragons, taking the outfield first, and the Red Warriors up to bat. Now, let the..." Mr. Roberts paused dramatically as he raised an arm and pointed at the campers and counselors in the stands.

"Games begin!" everyone shouted. The cheers continued as players took up their positions.

The crack of the bat, the cheering of the fans, and the satisfying thwonk of a ball landing perfectly in an open glove all became background noise to Marcus as he observed all the action Alissa was getting as the first-base coach while he, at third base, was getting none at all. Alissa clapped her hands, cheering on slow runners to move faster and overrun first base before the ball beat them to it. Two runners lost the race, but Alissa high-fived the kids anyway. Marcus smiled at this gesture, realizing how well Alissa worked with the younger kids, encouraging them even when they were down.

"Up next, Bri Kahale," Mr. Roberts announced through the PA. Marcus felt his stomach do a flip as his younger sister planted her feet firm and wide at the plate. Like Marcus, she didn't really like baseball. But over the summer, he and Alissa had worked with her on hitting and catching. Alissa, being one of those super athletic girls good at every sport, had pitched for her multiple times. After weeks of practice, Marcus had witnessed Bri consecutively send the ball sailing. He and Alissa knew Bri could hit a home run, even with two outs against them.

"You got this, girl!" Alissa shouted and clapped her hands.

Bri pointed her bat at Alissa. Alissa flashed a grin at Marcus, and he nodded.

As the pitch crossed the plate, Bri swung the bat and sent the ball flying. She dropped the bat and ran.

"Foul ball," Uncle Craig, a twenty-something counselor new this year, called. All senior counselors were referred to as Uncle or Aunt.

Bri, head up and tight-lipped, returned to home plate and took her stance. Another pitch came, and she swung.

"Streee-ike two," Uncle Craig called, emphasizing this with a swinging arc of his hand that ended with two of his fingers raised.

Uncle Craig seemed too into his role as umpire, Marcus observed. His sister shifted her feet and looked tiny compared to the older camper who was playing catcher. Marcus could tell Bri was getting psyched out.

"Hit it center field!" Marcus shouted. "Just like we practiced."

Bri nodded, adjusted her stance, and held the bat ready.

The next pitch was wide. Bri swung and missed. Uncle Craig called another strike.

"C'mon, Uncle Craig!" Alissa shouted. "It was wide! Where's your—"

The whistle blew.

Marcus didn't have to guess at the insult she intended to lob at Uncle Craig.

Alissa crossed her arms and frowned. The Red Warriors with much grumbling took the field, while the Blue Dragons with much cheering got ready to bat.

Bri, head down and glove dangling at her side, joined Marcus in the outfield.

"That sucked," she said.

"Nah." Marcus tousled her dark, tight curls.

Bri batted his hand away. Marcus knew she hated it when he tousled her hair, which was why he reserved it for moments like these.

"Seriously," Marcus said. "I would've done the same thing."

"I know. You suck, too." Bri punched him playfully in the arm as Alissa joined them.

"Can you believe that?" she asked indignantly. "I swear Uncle Craig is blind."

"No," Marcus said with a laugh. "He just left his glasses in the bunkhouse."

"Did he?" Bri asked.

"Nah," Alissa said. "You ready to catch?"

Bri gave her the stink eye. "Yeah, right. These kids can't hit a pop fly. But, just in case, I'm taking right field."

"Good luck," Marcus said.

Bri took off toward right field, where the ball was least likely to find its way.

"She'll be all right," Alissa said.

"Yeah," Marcus said. "You taught her well."

"We taught her well," Alissa corrected and flashed him a dimpled smile. "Well, see ya!"

"See ya," Marcus said. He watched Alissa run off to center field, then he took the sidelines.

Marcus sighed. Bri, though she was going into sixth grade at the end of the summer, was still one of the youngest kids staying overnight. Which was why it was so crucial for her to be in Alissa's cabin. The two girls were close. Alissa and Marcus, being the same age and next-door neighbors, had played together as they grew up. Alissa was an only child and treated Bri like the little sister she never had. He didn't mind that, but it did make

Alissa sort of like a sister to him. That, he thought, was definitely weird.

More cracks and cheering as one kid hit a grounder and ran toward first base. The ball rolled between the legs of the kid playing second base, and Bri was able to cover the play, tossing the ball to the boy on second base for an out.

"Nice one, Bri!" Marcus shouted.

Bri was far more practiced at catching balls than she was at hitting them. Marcus knew Bri would be fine if someone did hit a fly ball that came to her at just the right angle. He also knew most of the kids, boys and girls, batted right-handed. A few, the ones in Little League, could hit beyond the infield. But it was unlikely that the ball would go in Bri's direction.

Then, another kid, a lefty, was up to bat. He had that narrow-eyed glint of determination as he hugged home plate. When the bat connected with the ball, Marcus wasn't at all surprised that it went sailing toward right field. Bri raised her glove, but then turned away.

What is she doing? Marcus thought.

The ball flew over her head and landed somewhere in the woods that bordered the field. Bri looked around in surprise as the lefty rounded first base and made his way toward second. The Blue Dragons cheered; they were sure to get a home run if their runner hustled. Marcus ran toward Bri.

"What happened?" he asked.

Bri shrugged. "I don't know. I heard something in the woods."

"What do you mean something?" Marcus asked.

Bri pointed to the woods. "I think it was some branches rustling."

"It was probably just a deer," Marcus said. "Let's find our ball."

Bri cocked her head to the side and shrugged. "Okay."

Marcus and Bri were joined by Alissa. As they walked, Marcus tried not to think about how Nate would be bragging after the game for hitting a home run, even though he had nothing to do with it.

When they got to the tree line, Marcus noticed a lot of the trees were covered in poison ivy.

"How do you guys want to let this play out?" Alissa asked.

"We can't just leave the ball in there," Marcus said. "Mr. Roberts would have a fit if we lost a ball."

Alissa shook her head. "Nah, I don't think so. Not with all of this." She gestured toward the poison ivy.

"Hey, there's an opening!" Bri shouted. She crashed through the tree line before Marcus or Alissa could stop her. Marcus rolled his eyes.

"Geez, we should go after her," he replied.

"Yah think?" Alissa asked sarcastically and took off after Bri.

Marcus followed close behind. Alissa and Bri were peeking under brush and kicking up dry leaves. Marcus swiveled around, careful to scan the entire area until he spotted something round and white twenty yards away. He ran toward it.

As he bent down to pick up the ball, a flash of blue caught his attention. When Marcus glanced up, a man seemed to disappear through a thicket of trees. Marcus ran after him but stopped when he came to a faint trail. Though he'd been coming here for years, he couldn't recall ever seeing this pathway. He listened. Marcus' heart raced. He wondered if this man was the source of the noise that had distracted Bri. Without further thought, he ran after the man.

"Marcus, wait!" shouted Alissa. "Where are you going?"

Marcus stopped, looked, and listened. The man had disappeared, so Marcus returned to the girls.

"Did you guys see that?" he asked.

"See what?" asked Alissa. She raised an eyebrow while Bri shook her head.

Marcus shrugged. "I thought I saw some guy, but I don't know."

"Probably a runner," Alissa said. "These woods are a beautiful place for a jog."

"If you guys are done playing around," said Bri as she placed her hands on her hips, "there's still a game going on."

Alissa held up her hand, palm open, and winked at Marcus. "Yeah, stop playing around, Marcus."

Marcus tossed the ball to Alissa, and she caught it flawlessly. She turned and led Bri out of the woods.

"Just a runner," Marcus repeated as he exited the woods and rejoined the Red Warriors on the field. Though the camp was pretty secluded, and he'd never heard of anyone using these woods, the thought faded into oblivion as the heat of the day rose and the game reached a climactic fifth inning in which the Red Warriors and the Blue Dragons were neck and neck.

After the game, Marcus led his cluster of campers back to the bunkhouse. Ahead of him, Alissa put her arm around Bri as they walked toward their own bunkhouse. Janice joined Alissa and Bri in an animated conversation that Marcus couldn't make out, not from this distance and certainly not with all the campers around them.

"Hey," Nate said, catching up with Marcus and jabbing him in the side. "Blue Dragons smeared you guys today!" The Blue Dragons, led by Nate and Janice, had beat out Marcus' and Alissa's Red Warriors by five runs. Marcus looked at Nate, whose mop of curls was matted down with sweat.

"Yeah, some game," Marcus mumbled.

"Bro," Nate said. "Your team lost some steam after the fifth inning. What happened?"

"You just wait," Marcus said with a smirk. "We'll take you out in dodgeball."

Nate slapped Marcus on the back. "Only if you guys can beat the Orange Tigers in flag football."

"Not a problem." Marcus wriggled his eyebrows. "Alissa and I have a plan!"

Nate smiled and slowly nodded. "Is that what you guys were doing in the woods during the first inning?"

"Dude," Marcus said. "What're you getting at?"

Nate put his index finger to his lips and motioned toward the girls as they got closer.

Ignoring Nate's gesture, Marcus was about to say something to Nate until he heard Janice chatting excitedly about some boy, another junior counselor, she'd seen on the field. Marcus noticed Alissa half-listening, as her focus was on Nyah, another little girl.

Nate interrupted Marcus' thoughts. "You three were in the woods for a long time."

"Yeah, so?" Marcus asked with a shrug. He knew exactly what Nate was getting at. Since sixth grade, Nate had incessantly teased him about his thing for Alissa, but Marcus just as incessantly denied having a thing for Alissa.

"So," Nate added, "you wouldn't mind if someone else..."

Marcus let Nate continue uninterrupted with the same old teasing. It was fun and well intentioned, though irritating at times.

Marcus cringed when he heard Janice laugh.

"Alissa, you should go with Todd!" Janice squealed. "He'd probably ask you to the dance on Thursday night." She was referring to a corny luau-themed dance that Mr. Roberts and his wife hosted every year for all the campers.

"I don't think so," Alissa said to Janice. "Todd's definitely not my type."

Janice grabbed Alissa's arm. "Oooh! How about..."

Marcus hadn't asked anyone to the Thursday dance since he'd been in sixth grade. He hadn't thought to do so because he didn't really want to go with anyone except Alissa. He figured she'd say no since, growing up together, they were practically brother and sister. He was also worried it would make things super awkward between them later on, especially if things got serious and they suddenly broke it off. Instead, the past three years had consisted of Marcus wallflowering it at the dance while he watched Alissa enjoy herself with some other boy. Between this thought and the conversation going on in front of him, Marcus adopted a sullen look. He swallowed hard.

A sudden slap to his belly snapped Marcus out of his head. He glared at Nate, who was laughing hysterically. The girls, Marcus realized, had gone to get ready for swimming. He and Nate were standing still. Marcus had been staring at the girls' bunkhouse when Alissa, Janice, Bri, and the rest of the girls went inside. He and Nate were alone outside of their own rowdy bunkhouse.

"What's gotten into you?" Nate asked. He had a genuine look of concern on his face.

"I don't know." Marcus shook his head and tried to come up with some topic that didn't include Alissa. "Something happened in the woods."

Nate stepped closer. "Between you and Alissa?"

Marcus stared at Nate, wondering why his friend was whispering. "Huh? No, my sister was there and... What're you talking about?"

Nate shrugged and frowned. "I don't know. You're the one who's too chicken to ask her out."

Marcus blinked in surprise. Nate had always danced around the topic, and this direct approach was so sudden. Marcus wondered if Alissa or Janice had said anything to Nate. He wanted to pry Nate for further information.

"Maybe I am too afraid to ask Alissa out," Marcus said as he groaned. "What've you heard?"

"Oh," Nate said with a wink, "I heard a lot."

Oh, brother, Marcus thought. "And?"

"And the odds are definitely in your favor," Nate

said. "Go for it, lover boy, if you've got the guts. And, speaking of guts, Janice told me that Aunt Lauren said the 'haunted' cottage was torn down."

Aunt Lauren, being Mr. Roberts' daughter, would know things about the camp because she spent as much time here as her father. Naturally, some of her knowledge would trickle down to her junior counselors, Alissa and Janice.

"Okay," Marcus said. "So, what if the cottage is torn down?"

The cottage was located four miles into the woods. Marcus and Nate had ventured out there two summers ago. It was rumored that Mr. Roberts' father had died in the cottage, and his spirit haunted the place.

Nate shrugged. "I think it'll be fun to check it out."

"Do you think we'll find any old Roberts family relics?" Marcus asked.

Nate scratched the peach fuzz on his chin. "Maybe. I doubt it'll be as big of an adventure as it was two summers ago when your leg fell through a rotting floorboard. But I'm curious about what we'll find."

Though he wasn't terribly excited about the idea of seeing the place, Marcus knew Nate would go without him.

"So, tomorrow night?" Marcus asked.

Nate nodded, and his eyes twinkled with

mischief. Marcus grinned. Ever since they'd been campers here, Marcus and Nate would sneak out all the time. Nate would concoct some wild, covert operation and Marcus would follow. It was always a nice break from the routine of one activity after the next every day all summer long. Marcus was beginning to realize that being a junior counselor was no different than being a camper, only with more responsibility, and not nearly as much fun.

The bunkhouse door opened to thirteen noisy boys who should have been getting ready for their next activity, but Marcus relaxed at the thought of getting out with Nate and breaking some camp rules regarding curfew. Already, Marcus' anxiety over asking Alissa to Thursday's dance was giving way to the far more pleasing idea of a makeshift adventure that lay in wait for them around the bend of a dark trail in the middle of the night.

Chapter 2

Tuesday, July 17.

Alissa sat at the edge of her bunk on Tuesday afternoon as Aunt Lauren spoke to a fidgety group of girls. Alissa wasn't sure how long Aunt Lauren had worked the summers at camp, but she knew that Aunt Lauren was beginning her teaching career the first summer Alissa started as a day-camper, when she was nine years old. Alissa wasn't sure about Aunt Lauren's exact age, either. Her athletic build, shoulder-length hair pulled back in a ponytail, and permanent tan made her seem ageless. Like Alissa, Aunt Lauren never wore makeup, and she played in a soccer league.

"So, girls," Aunt Lauren said, "this week's

theme is growing our personal character."

Several hands rose. Aunt Lauren called on a strawberry-blonde-haired girl named Veronica.

"Don't we have campfire tonight?" Veronica asked.

"Yes," Aunt Lauren said. "But that's not really—"

"Ooh," another girl said. "Maybe you can tell us some stories about your grandfather's haunted old cottage."

"I don't think so," Aunt Lauren said. She bit her lower lip. "That's not really—"

"I heard," Veronica said, "that he died of a heart attack and that—"

"Girls." Alissa stood as she waved her hands to get their attention. "Aunt Lauren is trying to frame the week for you. Other talk can wait, okay?"

"Thank you, Alissa," said Aunt Lauren. She took a deep breath and went on. "Anyway, right now is a time to reflect on who you are. Perhaps one of our junior counselors would like to tell you about her experience when she was your age." Aunt Lauren gestured to Janice and Alissa. "Would either of you young ladies care to share?"

"Alissa would love to share," Janice replied too quickly. When Alissa shot her a glance, Janice's freckled porcelain skin turned a shade of pink. "I mean...she can begin. I'll add to her story as she goes along. Is that okay?" Janice's blue eyes were wide and pleading as she looked at Alissa.

Alissa knew that Janice, though she had no problem getting on stage to dance, sing, or act, hated public speaking. Despite being exceptionally talented, Janice lacked the confidence to lead a talk. Alissa smiled reassuringly at her friend.

"Sure, I'd love to," Alissa said. "Just jump in when you're ready."

Janice nodded, and her bob of short, black curls swayed.

Collecting her thoughts, Alissa made eye contact with each of the girls, losing herself for a moment in Bri's deep-set hazel eyes. Alissa never thought of herself as much of a public speaker, but she always found it was easier to stand in front of a group and talk if she could ground herself with someone she knew very well. Bri's smiling eyes were enough for Alissa to begin.

"As some of you know, Janice and I are best friends." Alissa paused and broke eye contact with Bri when a wave of giggles passed over the other girls. "I know. You wouldn't guess it because we seem to be opposites. You can see that just by the way we dress, or—"

"Of course, that's just the surface," said Janice as she cut Alissa off and stood. "But they represent our preferences. I mean, my outfit is the latest from Forever 21, well, except for the camp T-shirt, and she's wearing Adidas shorts and shoes. And—"

Alissa cleared her throat, distracting Janice from her talk. Alissa's cheeks grew hot. She hadn't expected Janice to jump in so soon, especially since Alissa hadn't made the essential points yet. She watched as Janice's eyes grew wide and her cheeks flushed. The campers giggled as they looked from Janice to Alissa until their laughter dwindled, leaving the room in a heavy silence.

Well, this is awkward, thought Alissa.

"And so," Aunt Lauren said, "these two young ladies show that you don't have to like all of the same things to be great friends."

"Right," said Janice as she looked at Alissa. "I mean, Alissa spends a lot of time with the soccer team and other sports. I spend a lot more time in drama club, dance, and poetry. It's crazy how we met, right?"

"Yeah," Alissa chimed in. She laughed, feeling more at ease. "We were terrible swimmers when we started camp. Then, we were the oldest ones in the beginners' level before we moved up."

Janice's head bobbed enthusiastically. "We called ourselves 'the floaters club' because that's all we could do."

"We are obviously interested in different things," Alissa continued, pulling her thoughts together. "But we've both been through experiences that tested our personal character. When I was in seventh grade, I was so super busy with practice and getting ready for the big game that I forgot to study for a science test. All the seventh-grade girls on the team were freaking out. Then, some of my classmates passed around copies of the test answers. One of the eighth-grade girls claimed our teacher never changed the test. I took the answers."

There was silence. Janice was staring wide-eyed at Alissa. Alissa realized she was telling a story that even Janice didn't know.

"Anyway, I was so tempted to just memorize the answers. I even looked at them a few times. But I couldn't bring myself to do it. The next day, I failed the test. The teacher found out about the cheating. I was even called into the principal's office. I told her I didn't know anything. But a few days later, I came back and showed them the answer sheet."

"So, you snitched?" asked one of the girls.

"Now, hold on," Aunt Lauren replied as she stood. "Snitching, compared to doing the right thing, is completely different. The point, though, is that your junior counselor's personal character was tested. She learned from her mistakes. Right, Alissa?"

Alissa nodded. "I learned to manage my time

better in the future, for one thing. For another, I swore I would never be in a situation like that again."

"Thank you, Alissa," Aunt Lauren said. She looked at the rest of the girls. "Here's your journal prompt for today. What qualities do you value in friends?"

Alissa sat back in her bunk. She could hear the gentle sounds of pencils jotting against notepads, breathing, and beds squeaking. Though she'd answered the question many times in her past overnight camping, Alissa pulled out her notebook and wrote. She valued friends who were reliable, honest, and always had her back. No matter what. She looked up and scanned the room, wondering what Bri, Nyah, and Janice were writing. Her eyes fell on Veronica, the strawberry blonde who had interrupted Aunt Lauren. Alissa gave her a slight wave, but the girl scowled back at her and returned to her own notebook. Alissa wondered what she'd done to offend the girl. She could think of nothing.

The seven-thirty evening bell rang, and Alissa and Janice inspected each of their campers as they headed out the bunkhouse into the chilly night air. Aunt Lauren, along with the other counselors, had gone up to prepare the fires a half hour ago, leaving junior counselors in charge of getting the kids properly dressed for the evening. Though they were in the middle of the summer, July in the Allegheny Mountains was chilly in the evening. Sweatshirts were required. Sweatpants or jeans were not. Alissa and Janice high-fived each girl who exited the bunkhouse properly dressed.

Bri and her friend Nyah were the first to exit without their sweatshirts on. Alissa held up a hand.

"And where do you two think you're going dressed like that?" she asked. She cringed inside when she finished her sentence, realizing how much she sounded like her mother.

"Do we have to change?" Bri asked in a whiny tone.

"C'mon," Nyah said as she pulled on Bri's shirt and sighed. "Let's go back in."

Alissa heard a commotion from the boy's cabin across the way. Still holding her hand up for the next high five, she turned and saw Marcus and Nate, doing pretty much the same with their boys. Alissa waved with her free hand and called to Marcus.

"Hey, you guys ready for the night?" she asked.

"Oh, yeah!" said Marcus as he rolled his eyes. "The boys are ready!"

"For s'mores!" Nate shouted back.

Marcus frowned. "Yeah, they weren't keen on the idea of a counselor skit on personal character."

"I know, right?" asked Alissa. She crossed her arms and laughed. For some reason, she realized she'd been shifting her weight from one foot to the other.

"Veronica, come back!" Janice shouted.

"Well, guess that's my cue," said Alissa. She waved to Nate and Marcus. "You guys have a good night."

Pivoting, Alissa saw Veronica, the strawberry-blonde girl, trotting away without a sweatshirt on.

"Hey, Veronica," called Alissa.

Veronica turned and sucked her teeth. "What?"

This little girl has a serious attitude, Alissa thought. Alissa allowed herself a few deep breaths before she calmly replied. "Your sweatshirt. You've forgotten it."

Alissa felt a small crowd gathering as Veronica crossed her arms and stared her down.

"I didn't forget it," she said flatly.

Alissa wasn't exactly sure how to answer this. Fortunately, Janice stepped forward, saving Alissa from having to immediately respond.

"Cute top," Janice said to Veronica. Then she quickly leaned in and whispered, "Veronica was giving me a hard time earlier. The rest are ready to go. Do you mind if I take them?"

Alissa grimaced. "Sure." Avoiding Veronica's glare, Alissa stared at the pink unicorn T-shirt the kid was wearing. Alissa didn't really want to be alone with Veronica, but she didn't want to hold anyone else back, either. When the rest of the girls were a safe distance away, Alissa tried to talk to Veronica again.

"Why don't you want to wear the sweatshirt?" she asked.

"I just don't!" Veronica yelled.

Alissa plopped herself on the bunkhouse steps and put her hand on her chin. "Well, you could run off and be cold for the rest of the night."

Veronica sneered. "Duh! We're going to be at a campfire."

"And there's going to be thirty kids. No one's going to be right next to the fire the whole night. You might be behind someone." Alissa shrugged. "Then what?"

Veronica bit her lip. "I just don't want to wear it, okay?"

"Okay," Alissa said. "Why not?"

Veronica turned away. "I can't wear it."

"Why?" Alissa looked at Veronica with concern and waited. "You can tell me." Alissa's voice was calm.

Veronica started to cry. "My mom...packed me a sweatshirt. But it's too...small." Veronica sniffled. "I don't have another one."

"No problem," Alissa said with a lilt in her voice. "You want to borrow one of mine? You can use it all week if you want."

Veronica nodded. Alissa was in and out of the bunkhouse in a flash. When she returned, she carried her favorite sweatshirt, a magenta Adidas pullover hoodie.

"Catch," she said as she tossed the hoodie to Veronica, who caught it.

"It's so soft!" Veronica exclaimed as she pulled the hoodie over her head.

"I know," Alissa said. "Race ya to Campfire?"

Alissa, though she could easily outrun Veronica, let her get ahead. Somehow, she doubted this would be her last encounter with the girl.

They caught up with their group sitting around a blazing bonfire. The firepit sat ten feet away from a stage. In a semicircle around the pit and in front of the stage, various seating options were available from logs to stumps to slabs of rocks. Alissa took a seat on a log next to Janice, who had saved her a place. Across from her, Marcus gave her a wave. Alissa waved back as Mr. Roberts, accompanied by Uncle Craig and Aunt Lauren, took the stage. Mr. Roberts waited for all the girls and boys to get settled.

"Now," he said, "tonight the counselors have prepared a skit." All the kids groaned, so Mr. Roberts held up his hand to quiet them. "The skit is titled 'Defined by Choices.'"

"Is this a comedy, or a horror?" asked a kid from

three rows back.

"Neither," Mr. Roberts said dryly. "But it'll be a horror if you interrupt again."

Alissa flinched at this comment, surprised that it would come from Mr. Roberts, a man who was usually pretty easygoing. She felt the tension among the campers and other staff members alike. She, like others, shifted in her seat as Janice, joined by Nate, took the stage.

As they took their places, Nyah's hand suddenly shot up, and she waved furiously until Mr. Roberts couldn't ignore it any longer.

"Nyah, do you have a question?" Mr. Roberts asked as he prepared to exit the stage and join the campers.

"Can I go to the bathroom?" asked Nyah. Her hand dropped, and her lower lip curled downward.

Mr. Roberts sighed. "Yes, take a buddy with you."

Nyah nodded and grabbed Bri's hand. "Let's go."

Alissa suppressed a laugh when Bri's pleading eyes met her own before she was practically dragged out of the circle. The girls seemed to disappear into the darkness where the fire could no longer cast its warm glow upon them.

When Mr. Roberts sat in the front row, the skit began as Janice, the one with the most stage experience at camp, took the stage. She paced back and forth, flailing her arms and offering a soliloquy about choosing between studying for a final exam or going out with her friends. She froze as Nate took the stage and, less dramatically, offered a monologue about breaking up. Similarly, other counselors joined the stage, doing their skits.

During one of the speeches, Alissa realized that Bri and Nyah had been gone for some time. With the bathroom so close by, they should've been back in under ten minutes.

Alissa stood up quietly to leave and walked through a fidgeting audience of campers, some of whom quickly turned their heads. Some frowned at her, while others narrowed their eyes. It was clear that they longed to be in her place, and Alissa didn't blame them. The skit, though better than a talk, was still cringy.

When Alissa passed the circle that made up the fire's glow, she flicked on her flashlight and followed the path to the bathrooms. A girl screamed suddenly in the night, and Alissa froze. The noise came from the bathrooms. She ran, the beam of her flashlight bouncing in front of her. Then, someone small collided with her. Alissa recognized the feel of the little girl's embrace.

"Nyah," Alissa said, nudging the girl away. "What's wrong?"

Nyah shook her head. "There's someone—"

"He's gone!" Bri shouted, pounding down the path.

"Who's gone?" asked a nasal male voice. The girls turned to see Mr. Roberts. "Girls, what did you see by the bathrooms?"

"I didn't see anyone." Nyah spoke first. "I was in the bathroom."

"I saw someone," Bri said hoarsely. Her voice cracked. "A man. He—"

"Okay," Mr. Roberts said quietly. "Alissa, take these two back to the campfire. We're going to round up all the kids."

"But, Mr. Roberts," Alissa began. "The girls were just about to—"

A muffled voice interrupted Alissa. Mr. Roberts was already turned away from her. He was talking into his handheld radio.

Alissa led Bri and Nyah back to the campfire, where they discovered everyone else was already filing out in an orderly fashion. Orderly, except for a few groans about missing s'mores.

Alissa let Janice lead the girls from the front, while she hung in the back to make sure there were no stragglers. She turned when she saw Bri and Nyah.

"Hey, Bri," Alissa whispered, "are you..."

Bri shook her head. This response, though not unfriendly, threw Alissa off for a moment and she wondered at its meaning.

When the last of the girls had exited, Alissa turned to Aunt Lauren, whose back was to her. She had a handheld radio to her ear. Mr. Roberts was nowhere in sight, and Marcus and Nate were helping Uncle Craig herd the campers to their bunkhouses. Alissa was desperate to stay back and eavesdrop on the conversation Aunt Lauren was having. Still, she didn't want to get reamed out, especially not after the earlier talk about personal character. Alissa decided it would be best to hurry Bri and Nyah back to the bunkhouse and follow up with Bri later in the evening.

As she caught up with her group, already merging with Marcus' and Nate's rowdy boys, Alissa noticed that Uncle Craig wasn't with them. She made a mental note to ask Aunt Lauren about whatever the heck had happened in the woods that would cause everyone to exit the bonfire and miss out on s'mores altogether.

Chapter 3

Alissa

Wednesday, July 18. 2:37 a.m.

Pssst... Pssst...

The bed shook, and so did I. Someone was whispering in my ear. With the faint glow of the moon peeking through the blinds, I could see only the shadowy form of a girl.

"Alissa, are you awake?" she asked softly.

She shook me, and I sat up. I rubbed my eyes and glanced at the digital clock by my bed. The time glowed a red two thirty-seven in the morning.

"I'm up now," I said. "What do you want, Bri?"

Bri was standing so close to me that I could feel and smell her hot breath.

"I need to tell you something about last night," she whispered.

Bri was bursting to talk. I'd tried to catch her alone a few times as we were getting ready for bed, but Aunt Lauren's constant presence and the understandable excitement in the room didn't let that happen. I could tell then, like now, that Bri had something crazy to say to me.

"Sit here," I said, patting my bed. "But keep it down. We don't want the other girls waking up."

She scooted close to me, the way my cat at home did when the weather was cold. Bri snuggled her tiny, bony frame against me. For the longest time, I thought she wouldn't say anything at all.

"You remember when we came from the bathroom?" she asked.

I nodded, even though she couldn't see me. "Yeah."

"There was…" She squirmed and then laid her head on my lap with a whimper. "Someone else was in the woods."

"Was that you screaming?"

Bri nodded.

I gulped. "Did this someone grab you?"

Bri shot up. "No!"

"Quiet!" exclaimed someone on the other side

of the cabin. Then, we heard shushing from somewhere else. Bri leaned toward me and lowered her voice.

"So, about that guy," Bri continued. "I think I scared him more than he—"

The front door popped open.

"Girls, you need to be quiet now," said Aunt Lauren as she entered the cabin. "It's past three in the morning." Aunt Lauren kept watch during the last part of the night. Her athletic frame, silhouetted by the glow of a lamp, cast a shadow on the floor.

"What are you doing up?" Aunt Lauren asked in one of those whispers that was not really a whisper but more like a raspy yell. She walked to my bed. "Alissa, you should be leading by example."

"Oh," I paused. "Bri was just—"

"I wasn't feeling well," interjected Bri, who scooted to the edge of the bed. "So, I came over here."

The girl's quick, I thought.

Aunt Lauren stood there with her hands on her hips, scrutinizing us. I wasn't sure why Bri didn't tell her about the man in the woods. Aunt Lauren glanced between Bri and me. She waited for an explanation, and I decided I would wait on Bri to be ready to tell the rest of her story. Aunt Lauren knelt until she was eye level with Bri.

"Let's talk in the bathroom, okay?" she asked. Aunt Lauren turned and walked away. When Bri didn't follow, I gave her a little push off the bed to go with Aunt Lauren.

In the light of the bathroom, Bri stood before Aunt Lauren while giving her best pout. I strained to make out their whispers as Bri held her stomach. Aunt Lauren put the back of her hand to Bri's forehead. If I hadn't known the truth, I would've bought the act myself.

Chapter 4

Marcus

4:15 a.m.

Stretched out and limbs spread wide, I lay on top of my open sleeping bag. I hadn't slept for most of the night, and that was not because I was wearing a T-shirt, sweatpants, and socks. No, I was waiting and listening for the end of the night shift.

When Nate and I were returning to the bunkhouse after campfire was cut short, he passed me and told me tonight would be even more interesting. I thought he was being a little callous, since Bri was clearly freaked out about something that she saw. But I let it go, knowing that she'd be in good hands with Alissa and that I'd get the details in the morning.

The bunkhouse door opened, and a flashlight sought the dark corners of the room. Its owner, satisfied that all were accounted for, killed the light and shut the door, leaving us all in the dark once again.

I hopped out of my bunk and landed with a thud. I took a creaky step toward the window and peeked through the blinds. The night watchman was heading in the direction of the Roberts house, which was positioned on a knoll near the front entrance of the camp.

A tap on my shoulder made me turn. In the moonlight, Nate's disheveled hair and a wild look in his eyes told me he was ready to boil over with some crazy scheme he'd been cooking up while everyone was supposed to be asleep.

"Bro," Nate whispered. "You ready?"

I nodded. "The night watch just left. See." I held the horizontal blind open as Nate took my place.

"I know," he said. "Listen. There's something else."

We held our breath. I could hear crickets and the rustling of bushes. The rustling didn't sound close. Not like you hear when a counselor is trying to freak you out by shaking the bushes and trees around the cabin or by occasionally pounding on the walls. No, this was different. And it came from Cabin Six, the girls' cabin across the gravel pathway.

"Think we should check it out?" I asked, glancing at the clock on the wall. "I mean it's past four in the morning."

"Time's never been an issue before," said Nate with a shrug. "Let's do it."

Ever since we had been campers here, he and I would sneak out some nights, pretending to be detectives on a high-stakes case. Even at age sixteen, the idea still excited me. So, I popped my feet into my slip-ons and followed Nate. Like me, he was already dressed and ready for adventure.

"Wait up," I whispered. Nate held the door open just enough, so it wouldn't creak as we exited.

In the moonlight, we could see only the shadows of things: trees, electrical wires, and decorative boulders. Then, the creak of a door echoed among the trees. We ducked into a bush and watched movement from the girls' cabins. Two adults, one significantly taller than the other, passed on the far side of the adjacent bunkhouse. The shorter one had something lumpy, like a bag of dirty laundry, thrown over his left shoulder.

Beside me, Nate shifted and the bush we had been using as cover rustled.

The taller of the adults, a man, looked around and stopped when he faced our direction. He stared me down, or it felt like he did, for a long time. Then he turned, gestured to the shorter one with the sack, and the two disappeared into the shadows.

"Follow me," Nate whispered. Before I could protest, he crouched and ran across the path and flattened himself against the adjacent bunkhouse. I did the same.

"Are you crazy?" I asked between breaths. Nate smirked and nodded, and he was off again.

I followed him like that until we were crouching at the edge of a thin treeline that overlooked the soccer field. Beyond the field, we saw the two figures pass the white ring of light glowing on the basketball courts. They stopped and looked around. I caught the profile of the taller figure. He might have been around eighteen, with a short unkempt beard.

"Do you recognize that guy?" I asked.

Nate shook his head. "Too far away to tell. But I don't think I've seen him before. Maybe he's maintenance?"

"Maybe he is," I said. "That would explain the sack the other guy's carrying."

"Yeah." Nate rubbed his chin. "What if there's a body in that bag?"

I flinched. "What?"

Nate shrugged. "Just trying to set the mood. You know, add a little flair."

I punched Nate lightly on the shoulder. "Good one. Maybe we'll spoil their dastardly deed."

Nodding, Nate rose. We closed the distance between ourselves and the two men, who by now had flicked on a flashlight. The beam of light started to shrink into the darkness beyond the basketball courts. I turned toward Nate, only to blink rapidly as a light flashed on beside him.

"They're headed through the baseball field," whispered Nate as he pointed his flashlight. "There's nothing beyond that but the woods."

"Geez, turn that off," I hissed through clenched teeth. "You want those guys seeing it?"

Nate adjusted the light until it radiated a soft glow. "Good thing I brought it. They're headed into the woods. Right where we wanted to go." Nate flailed his flashlight excitedly. "Let's go before we lose them!"

Before I could respond, Nate darted across the field. I ran after him, and soon we could see the glow of the men's flashlight veiled by the thicket of the woods ahead of us.

Once we were in right field, I took my flashlight from my pocket and swept the treeline in search of the pathway I'd seen during Monday's baseball game. My heart was racing, and not just from the running. I could never sleep on nights we were going to sneak out of our bunkhouse. Nate never told me everything he had planned. That was what made it exciting. But we'd never chased anyone through the woods at night, and I was pretty certain he was making this part of the plan up as we went along.

"Here's the entrance," I said. "Watch out for poison ivy."

As we stepped through the woods, I could no longer see the flashlight beam from the two men ahead of us. I was passing my flashlight along the ground, when another circle of light joined mine.

"Turn it off," I said. "We don't want to get caught."

"Turn it off yourself," Nate hissed. "There's a path ahead."

I grinned, holding the flashlight to my face mischievously. "What'd you do? Go down here during break today?"

Nate chuckled. "Something like that." He moved forward. "C'mon, I know the way."

Following the pathway illuminated by Nate's flashlight, I watched my feet. The ring of light on the ground was small, but I could tell this path wouldn't even be easy to walk through during the day—not with so many roots, the loose gravel, and the incline.

Suddenly, I slipped on some loose gravel and skidded onto my butt with a yelp. Then I was blinking dark spots out of my eyes in the brightness of what felt like a searchlight.

"I told you we were being followed," a man's voice squeaked.

"What're you two kids doing out?" asked another man with a deeper, calmer voice than the first.

Before I could answer, Nate grabbed me and pulled me up and then toward the camp. I didn't look back. We tripped and fell a few times as we made our getaway. After a few minutes, we decided they weren't coming after us. If they were, they would have caught us already.

When we reached the clearing of the baseball field, we retraced our steps from shadow to shadow, not stopping until we reached our bunkhouse. We didn't even try to keep the door from making noise as we creaked it open and slammed it behind us. We kicked off our shoes and buried ourselves deep inside our sleeping bags.

Moments later, the cabin door reopened. Someone was standing there, scanning the room. I couldn't tell if it was someone from the night watch, or one of the two men, or if they were somehow one and the same. But I heard a shoe scuff on the floor as the intruder searched the room. He stopped right by my bed. I could hear the guy breathing heavily.

I had a sudden urge to punch the guy, just so his hot breath would stop hovering over me. I couldn't imagine a scenario in which that would make any kind of sense. I tried to breathe steadily and slowly, like I was asleep. I moved slightly, like I was stretching, and the man moved on.

The heavy breathing and the scuffing of the shoes faded away until I heard the door creak open. Slowly, the door latched closed with a click. There was no way of knowing if this guy had really left, or if he was pretending, so he could catch someone awake. I'd heard stories of the night watch doing that. The next day, the kid who was caught awake would be sent home for causing a disruption. That wouldn't be me.

"Yo," a kid whispered too loudly. "What was that?"

"Nothing," a man's deep, calm voice came. "Go back to bed. You kids play around too much."

I recognized the man's voice from the woods, and it confirmed we had been followed after all. The door opened again, and this time I knew the man had left. Everyone returned to sleep, except for me.

I couldn't sleep after that.

Chapter 5

Alissa

6:45 a.m.

Last night, Aunt Lauren had taken Bri to get some medicine for her stomachache. After that, I don't really remember sleeping. I'm sure I dozed off, but that dreaded recording of a trumpet blasting "Reveille" came too early. It was followed by Aunt Lauren yelling at us to wake up. Janice shook the girls, who still seemed groggy, then came over to me with a wide grin on her face.

"I'm up," I groaned. Janice shook the bed anyway.

"Sorry, not sorry!" she sang. She was too awake and too dressed up this early. She wore a pink, low-cut T-shirt that showed off her flat tummy every time she raised her arms, and frayed jean shorts with an inseam far shorter than the allowed six inches.

"You're going to wear that?" I asked, scrunching my face. "What happens if Mr. Roberts catches you?"

"Meh," she said with a shrug. "That's a big if. Roberts hardly notices anything."

"Well, I wouldn't be caught dead wearing that." I sat up. "Not with my bubble butt and these." I waved my hands over my chest.

"Seriously." Janice smirked and plopped herself on my bed. "Your wardrobe consists of soccer shorts and jerseys from every team you've played on since you were, like, in the second grade." She leaned toward me, and a waft of her sweet, floral fragrance almost made me choke.

I placed a knuckle to my nostrils, trying not to inhale her perfume. "I stopped growing in the sixth grade, so..."

"So, what?" Janice poked my tummy and started tickling me. We laughed, and I could taste the bittersweet scent of jasmine, lily of the valley, vanilla and whatever else was in the perfume Janice was wearing. She sat back, supporting her weight on the heels of her hands, and tilted her head. "You're hot, so stop hiding what your momma gave ya!"

I chuckled at my best friend's corny line and climbed out of bed. Her perfume seemed to follow me, and I wrinkled my nose.

"Did you raid your grandmother's vanity?" I asked as I pinched my nose.

"No," she said with a wink. "It's Chanel No 5. Get ready." She tossed her short, dark curls as she stood. "You're going to be late for breakfast."

Janice sauntered off to wake the owner of a mop of tangled blonde hair sticking out from a lumpy sleeping bag. I bent down, pulled out my suitcase, and began to sift through my collection of soccer gear, looking for a T-shirt and shorts that matched well enough. I knew what Janice was doing, or trying to do to impress a boy, but she didn't know Marcus like I did. He didn't like all that girly stuff.

Marcus. That's when I remembered his little sister. Bri would have had a horrible night, based on what she told me. I ran over to her bunk to check on her before anyone else could, but her bed was empty.

"Hey, Janice," I called. "Where's Bri?"

"Hmmm…" said Janice, then shrugged. "Maybe she's in the bathroom. Let me check."

Janice checked the bathroom and came out almost instantly. "She's not in here. Shower stalls are empty, too. If you want a shower, you'd better hurry."

"That's weird," I said, getting up and grabbing a wad of clothes and my toiletries. "Bri would—"

"Ten minutes, ladies!" Aunt Lauren hollered as she came in the room amid a flurry of campers attempting to tidy their bunks. "Ten minutes and we're lining up outside for inspection!"

"Hey," I said to Aunt Lauren as she walked by, "where's Bri?"

Aunt Lauren looked me up and down, clearly deflecting my question. "Are you going to breakfast like that?" She paused.

I suddenly felt naked even though I wore an extra-large T-shirt that fell far past my silk night shorts. The night shorts were a gift from Janice. Aunt Lauren, wearing her crisp white Camp Lenape polo, crossed her arms and stood there as if waiting for an answer.

"You better get into that bathroom, Alissa," she demanded. "You're setting a bad example."

Before I could respond, she left me there, still wondering about Bri. She began to pester a hapless girl who was having a hard time stuffing a wad of clothes in a tiny duffel bag. I draped my towel over my shoulder, grabbed my clothes and toiletries, and dashed into the bathroom. I ended up cutting in front of a girl who was about to step into a shower stall.

"Hey," the girl whined.

"JC privileges," I replied and slammed the stall shut, locking it behind me.

As the water in the shower warmed up, I put my hair in an updo to keep my braids dry. Checking the shower temperature with satisfaction, I got in and thought about my exchange with Aunt Lauren. I couldn't help but feel like something was off. As far as I knew, I hadn't done anything wrong for Aunt Lauren to be getting on my case. I mean, I thought I knew her pretty well. I'd been a camper under her leadership for years, and I was so looking forward to working with her this summer. When I was a camper, she was my counselor for many years. I thought being her junior counselor would be great, but now I wasn't so sure.

With my shower finished, I hopped out, dried off, got dressed, and spritzed on coconut-vanilla body spray, my favorite scent. When I stepped out of the shower stall, my breath caught in my throat as I heard absolute silence from the bunk room.

"Hey, guys," I called.

Receiving no reply, I poked my head out of the bathroom and glanced around. All but two of the beds, my own and another, were made and the areas were inspection ready.

I was going to be in so much trouble. I must've

taken too much time in the shower, and that was a luxury no camper, and certainly no junior counselor, could afford. I tossed my toiletries, towel, and pajamas on my unmade bed and walked to the door. I closed my eyes and took a deep breath to brace myself for Aunt Lauren's yelling again.

I opened the door to the morning air, thick with humidity that stuck to my bare skin.

Chapter 6

Marcus

7:05 a.m.

I rolled over for what felt like the hundredth time, trying to block out the noise of campers preparing to leave. When I got the feeling someone was close by, I opened my eyes. Nate greeted me with a grin.

"Dude, the others are already up," he said.

I climbed out of bed slowly, not hopping down like I usually did. Really, I didn't feel like doing much at all. The campers were already pushing each other. Uncle Craig, the senior counselor, was barking at them to hurry up in the bathrooms. All but a couple of the boys were ready to go, even though I knew most of them hadn't showered for the second day in a row.

Uncle Craig leaned his muscular, tall frame against the bathroom doorway. He was new this year, and I'd heard he recently came in third place in a triathlon. The campers seemed impressed by him. I looked forward to testing myself against him in a sprint. As he shifted his attention from bathroom to bunk room, Uncle Craig swept his blond hair out of his eyes. He barked orders to a kid holding up the line at the sink. Nate followed me into the bathroom as we both brushed by Uncle Craig.

"Glad you're up," Uncle Craig said. "You two take over in here while I check on the boys in the sleeping quarters."

"Okay," Nate said.

Uncle Craig turned and went into the bunk room as I entered a stall.

"Time's up, boys," said Nate, shooing away a couple of campers. Finished, I exited the stall and saw Nate leaning against a sink. The bathroom door was closed. We were alone. I opened my mouth to speak, but Nate shushed me.

"Why'd you do that?" I asked.

"Hold on a sec," Nate whispered. He turned on the faucet. "Who do you think those men were last night?" Nate asked.

I raised my eyebrow. "Why are we so secretive?"

"It's happening." Nate's hands started to jitter. "We've got a real case this time."

I was exhausted, and my rear end was sore from losing my footing last night. Still, I shared Nate's curiosity. He had enough enthusiasm for the both of us. For the moment, I decided to entertain the idea of a case.

"That was a huge bag that guy was carrying," I said as I washed my hands.

"Yeah," Nate said. He handed me a couple of paper towels. "But where were they taking it? Why not take the bag to the dumpster? It's near the front of the camp and in the opposite direction of the woods. And that dude who walked in last night. I didn't get a good look at him because it was too dark. He was right next to your bunk. Did you get a look at him?"

"No, I was too far under my covers," I said. I tossed the wet paper towels into the wastebasket. As I reached for the door to leave the bathroom, Nate blocked my path.

"Wait," he said. "Who do you think he was?"

"Probably some guy the camp hired," I replied. "Maybe he was just doing his job." I elbowed Nate playfully. "You know, making sure no one was running around the camp."

"I guess so," Nate said, "but do you think those other guys were following us?"

I pursed my lips. "Yeah, I think they were. That guy who came into our cabin last night sounded like one of the guys who found us in the woods."

Nate face-palmed his forehead. "You're right. He did sound a lot like him. I'm just trying to piece this together. I don't get why he would follow us."

"Just drop it, for now, okay?" I raised my hands in the air. "I'm tired. We've got to head out to inspection and breakfast."

Nate turned off the water. "Don't worry about inspection. Before I woke you up, I told Uncle Craig you weren't feeling good. He took the others to the mess hall." He opened the door. "See, no one's here."

"Impressive," I said with a nod, looking around at the empty, but messy, bunkhouse. "I think I'm going to hang back here for a bit."

"You know..." Nate paused.

"What is it?" I asked.

He stepped forward. "Last night, I saw the man..."

I wasn't sure where this was going, but I knew I didn't like it. "What? Nate, tell me."

"I don't know, man. I mean, that guy was, like, standing over you. It was really weird."

"It was nothing," I said as I pushed past him.

"C'mon, bro. The way you're acting, you'd think he—"

"Nothing," I cut Nate off. "All I heard was his

heavy breathing like he'd been running hard."

Nate nodded. "And he hung there like a stale fart. What was his deal?"

I shook my head. "I don't know. Go ahead without me. I'll catch up, okay?"

"You sure? I mean—"

"Go," I said a little too forcefully. Nate ran. I plopped myself on the bunk underneath mine and put my hands on my face. I'd never had a strange man, or anyone for that matter, hang over me like that. Between what we'd seen last night and this guy who managed to catch up to us, I didn't know what to make of this place I used to look forward to every year. I was beginning to wonder, just the third day into a month-long gig, whether I'd made the right choice about being a junior camp counselor.

Chapter 7

Alissa

7:15 a.m.

Outside the cabin, the humidity not only clung to my skin, but I could smell hints of rain in the air. I wasn't as late as I thought. The girls were lined up in rows, holding up their hands, palms down so that Aunt Lauren and Janice could inspect their fingernails. Some of the girls, like Bri, would likely be sent back in to clean their hands again and pay special attention to the grit beneath their nails. I frowned. I didn't see Bri anywhere. But I did see Aunt Lauren staring at me.

"So nice of you to join us, Alissa," she proclaimed. "Don't you look refreshed?"

I winced. I didn't like Aunt Lauren's sarcasm. Behind her, Janice was shaking her head while mouthing something that looked like She's crazy this morning.

I squinted and craned my neck forward, trying to get her to say more. The other girls were looking at Janice. Aunt Lauren glanced at her as well, and then back at me.

"Alissa, we're missing someone," Aunt Lauren said. "Did you see her?"

"Are you talking about Bri?" I asked as I approached her.

Aunt Lauren gave a tight smile. "She went home. But I wasn't talking about her. I was talking about Nyah."

"Oh." I wasn't sure what else to say. I felt stupid as I bowed my head. "Let me get on that."

I let the door slam shut behind me as a storm of anger and confusion raged within me. Aunt Lauren wasn't telling me anything. Janice seemed to think she was nuts. Now, I had to find Nyah. Maybe she'd know what had happened to Bri. But I doubted it.

Nyah was still a mound buried in her sleeping bag when I found her. I tried to wake her by gently shaking the bed. When that didn't work, I shook the bedframe more violently. She still didn't respond, so I yanked off her sleeping bag. Nyah rose with a groan and dragged herself to the bathroom. As she cleaned up, I kept telling her to move faster, but that seemed to slow her down. After she showered and got dressed, she leaned over the sink to brush her teeth. While she was preoccupied, I figured I might as well make the best of my predicament and get some answers. So, I began my interrogation.

"Hey, Nyah," I said nonchalantly. "You're friends with Bri, right?"

"Yeah, why?" she asked in a muffled voice. She spat a stream of foam into the sink.

"Do you know where she is?"

"No." She stiffened. "Why would I know that?"

I inched closer to her. "Tell me about what happened when you two went to the bathroom."

She stood upright, erect like a prairie dog looking over a desert, a dusty and dangerous desert. Nyah spat again even though she didn't have any more toothpaste in her mouth.

"Bri got lost," Nyah blurted.

"What about the scream in the woods?" I asked as I narrowed my eyes.

Nyah shook her head, rinsed her mouth, and spat out the water. "We should go. I'm hungry, aren't you?" She dried her hands and mouth with a paper towel. Suddenly, she was moving past me. I had to speed walk so that I could follow her out of the cabin and toward the mess hall.

We opened the door at the worst possible time. Mr. Roberts began his morning speech at seven thirty sharp. It was seven twenty-nine, and no one was ready to listen. The pale and paunchy old guy rushed between groups, trying to keep his speech on schedule. He hushed the kids and counselors alike. Then, he spotted us.

"Hey, you two!" he shouted over the dying din. "Glad you could make it, Alissa and uh..." Mr. Roberts squinted at Nyah. "Hey, sweetie, what's your name?"

Nyah rolled her eyes and gave me one of those is-he-serious looks. She sucked her teeth. "My name is Nyah," she said flatly.

"Now, c'mon," Mr. Roberts said. "That's rude. We don't suck our teeth at Camp Lenape, do we, campers?"

"No," chimed all the kids in earshot, like a cult.

"Why don't you two sit there?" Mr. Roberts pointed to a random table.

I opened my mouth to speak, but he turned away from us and continued to talk, paying Nyah and me no more mind. Mr. Roberts was usually a meticulous guy who liked everything in order, including where everyone sat, so it was odd of him to place us just anywhere. Ignoring his directive, we snuck to our own table. Nyah slid next to a group of girls, and I scooted into a seat beside Janice.

"Hey," Janice whispered. "Everything okay?"

I shook my head. "Something's up. Have you heard anything about Bri?"

"Yeah," she said. "Aunt Lauren said she went home sick."

"What did she—"

"Alrighty now," Mr. Roberts shouted. He took a deep breath and smiled. "Well...it's a..." He raised his right hand as if he were a church cantor, and we were the congregation.

"Beautiful day at Camp Lenape," said some of the kids in unison. Everyone was expected to join in saying the greeting, but only half of the campers did. Their voices were scattered throughout the mess hall. Mr. Roberts ignored the campers' disobedience as he began the day's agenda. In turn, most of the campers ignored him because their stomachs were growling as they thought about their food getting cold.

While Mr. Roberts was still going on about today's activities, the door opened again. The campers glanced away as if they were grateful for the distraction and then returned their attention to Mr. Roberts. As for me, I couldn't look away. Marcus, unusually late, stood in the doorway. His downcast eyes and the way he plopped himself on the bench next to the door told me he was upset.

Chapter 8

Marcus

7:35 a.m.

After I sat down, I tuned Mr. Roberts out entirely and began to scan the room. I hoped to spot one of the men from last night. First, I saw Nate looking at me with one of those dude-you-okay looks. I gave him a lame thumbs-up and continued my search. I stopped again when Alissa's gaze caught mine. Her eyebrows were drawn together. There was something about the way her eyes seemed to pierce through me. I knew something was seriously wrong.

I looked down. I was tired. That was all. But I couldn't put Alissa's eyes out of my mind. I snuck a look at her and sighed. Her attention was back on Mr. Roberts.

From where I was sitting, I needed to get a sense of everyone else in the room. Everyone seemed normal—like nothing had happened last night. I thought at least a few of them would have heard the two men we followed through the woods. The only ones who seemed off were Alissa and Nate. I knew why Nate was off. For some reason, he was waving a hand at Alissa like he was trying to get her attention, but she was looking at me now and gesturing to another part of the room. I looked, trying to follow her gesture. I realized that my sister Bri was missing. She probably went to the bathroom, I thought. She tended to disappear like that.

Then I saw Janice waving at me. She was almost too excited, like she hadn't seen me in forever, even though we were at campfire last night. Janice wasn't the kind of girl to get excited about camp. And what was with her outfit and makeup? Weirdo.

I shrugged, looked back at Alissa, and raised an eyebrow. She was mouthing something to me. I couldn't make it out.

Alissa rolled her eyes and tapped Janice on the shoulder. Janice turned. Alissa cupped a hand over her mouth and whispered something. Nodding vigorously, Janice pantomimed a gagging gesture. I shook my head and pointed behind them at Mr. Roberts who, continuing with his speech, was approaching Janice. Mr. Roberts crossed his arms and cleared his throat.

"Would you two care to share the joke?" he asked.

"Sorry!" Janice apologized and shook her head. "I had a bit of...something...stuck in my throat."

"Are you okay?" Mr. Roberts asked. "Do you need anything?"

"She's okay," Alissa said. "She can wait."

Mr. Roberts eyed them both for a moment, then continued talking as he walked away. Some kids snickered. I turned away and stifled a laugh. Something was clearly up, but I couldn't figure it out, not with Alissa's and Janice's poor attempt at charades.

Mr. Roberts' speech continued for a moment longer about the day's exciting activities until he called the first table. Kids began to line up. I remained where I was until my usual table was called, and I joined them at the back of the line. After another group rose, I felt a tap on my shoulder and turned to see Alissa. I blinked. I couldn't avoid her any longer: the way her eyes reflected the light as she gazed at me, her dimpled cheeks as she gave me a tight-lipped smile.

"Hey," Alissa said quietly. "You okay?"

"I'm fine," I said. "Why?"

Alissa hesitated. "It's about your sister. She went home sick last night."

"What do you mean?" I stared at her, waiting for an explanation.

"You didn't hear?" She raised her voice, like she was trying to wake the dead, or simply talk over the buzz of over a hundred starving kids who would be disappointed at another cold meal. Suddenly, Alissa jolted forward, almost spilling her tray onto my shirt. Almost because I caught the tray. She turned and we were both looking at one of the campers. He was a small boy about Bri's age.

"Can you chill out?" Alissa practically yelled at the little kid.

The boy stumbled away from Alissa. His eyes glistened as if he were going to cry.

Some of the senior counselors looked our way. One of them, Uncle Craig, bounced out of his seat. He was approaching us, but Mr. Roberts seemed to appear out of nowhere. He signaled for Uncle Craig to sit.

"Hey, guys," Mr. Roberts said in the nasally voice he sometimes used to sound less threatening. "What's going on here?"

"I'm sorry," Alissa said. "We were moving too slow."

"Well..." Mr. Roberts gave an exasperated sigh as he paused. "Alissa, as a junior counselor, you should know better. At Camp Lenape, we say, 'Excuse me,' not...chill out." He made air quotes with his fingers on the last two words and peered around the mess hall. "Isn't that right, kids?"

"Yes, sir," replied some of the kids. Mr. Roberts deflated a little at hearing only a handful of kids reply.

"All right, you guys be good now," Mr. Roberts said with his nasal voice again. He shuffled off.

"Tell me what happened," I said as the line began to move.

Alissa relayed everything she knew—about the strange man approaching Bri and Nyah, and Bri pretending to be sick. Alissa concluded that Bri was trying to avoid getting caught, but she didn't know why.

"That is really strange because Nate and I saw something last night," I replied, omitting the part about pretending to be detectives. I told her about the two guys we followed last night and about how they were carrying something large through the woods.

"What the heck!" Alissa said. "Every year, you and Nate keep sneaking out without us."

I swallowed. "I'm sorry. I didn't—"

Alissa chuckled. "I'm teasing." She stepped closer and winked. "Just don't let it happen again."

"I won't," I said. "So, about those guys we saw?"

"Weird time for guys to be working in the woods?" Alissa offered. "But maybe not with Mr. Roberts' little quirks."

We both laughed.

"Anyway, if Bri were sick, the nurse would've sent her home. I'm just surprised you haven't heard anything about her leaving, yet. Normally, they'd tell us stuff like that."

I chewed my lower lip for a moment. "Maybe it was really bad."

"Nah. Bri was faking it." Alissa frowned and brushed a lock over her ear. "Even if she did suddenly get sick, your guys running around in the woods are completely unrelated."

"Or maybe..." My voice trailed off as we arrived at Alissa's table.

"Or maybe," Alissa repeated. "Maybe you should talk to Mr. Roberts. You know, call home."

"I guess," I said, kicking the toe of my shoe into the floor. I wasn't convinced.

Alissa placed a hand on my shoulder and looked me in the eyes. "Look, Bri's gone home. That's what Aunt Lauren told Janice. It's weird the way it was handled. But we've been going to this camp for too many summers. It's all about integrity and personal character. Why would they go against that?"

I sighed. "You're right. I guess I'll go back to my table and call my parents after breakfast."

Alissa nodded. "Definitely. Sucks we can't just use our cell phones."

"Ah, man!" I exclaimed. "Sucks that cell reception is nonexistent around here."

Alissa chuckled. "When do you think you're gonna go?"

I paused for a moment. "I guess I'll head to Mr. Roberts' house to use the phone after Nate takes our campers to the pool." I shifted a foot and cleared my throat. "Do you want to come with me?"

"If you want me to, sure," Alissa said.

"Really?" I asked a little too eagerly. "I mean, cool."

We took our seats. I picked at my food, though I was glad that Alissa would be coming with me. Occasionally, I glanced over my shoulder to see her. A few times, we caught each other's eyes. She wasn't eating anything. We both knew something strange was going on. We just couldn't put our fingers on it.

Chapter 9

Alissa

8:15 a.m.

Ugh, Kitchen Patrol duty, I thought. KP was the worst part of the week. Janice and I, as junior counselors, had to stay with our girls to clean the entire mess hall because Wednesday breakfast was always Cabin Six's turn. Meanwhile, the other junior counselors and their campers returned to their cabins. The senior counselors had their morning meeting.

Wednesday breakfast was the messiest and had always had the most leftovers ever since I was a camper here. We always complained about Wednesday breakfast. Even our parents, who didn't have to eat it or see it, complained. I didn't understand how the kitchen staff could think kids wanted to choose between room-temperature creamed chipped beef and thick, cold sausage gravy for breakfast.

So, the cleaning began. I predicted thirteen girls would scurry around, splashing water on each other, as they dropped rags into water buckets. Then, they would slop their rags onto tables, dropping crumbs of beef and sausage gravy onto the floor. They would laugh at the mess they made while forcing another girl, who had just swept under the table, to do it all over again. The cleanup process would be brutal.

There would be so much noise: chattering, giggling, and...dawdling. Stop dawdling, my mom used to say. She told me that when I got up in the morning, but of course, I wouldn't stop.

Just like I did when I was a kid, I knew these girls would dawdle and completely ignore any threat or incentive I'd call out to make them work faster. I thought they would be loud, except today, they dawdled in silence.

"Janice, you notice anything different?" I asked.

"Nope," she said as she stared at her reflection in a handheld mirror. She turned her face from side to side and puckered her lips.

I groaned. "You're not even paying attention!"

She snapped her mirror shut and shoved it into her back pocket. "Am too. You asked if I noticed anything different." She gave me a hard look. "I don't. You look the same as always. Braids. Maybe a few new beads. Soccer shorts. T-shirt. Seriously, we've got to get you a new wardrobe. And whoops..." She grabbed a wet rag and whipped it on my cheek. "A bit of schmutz on your face."

"Eww, that stinks! Get it away." I swiped at her hand.

"You're welcome." Janice grinned and tossed the rag into a bucket that one of our girls was carrying past us.

"I wasn't talking about me," I said as I huddled closer to Janice. "I was talking about the girls. Don't they seem different?"

"Well..." She paused and briefly surveyed the room. "This place is kind of a drag."

"Yeah," I said absentmindedly. "I wonder if it's because Bri is missing."

"That could be why. I mean, a spider bit her, which is a big deal. Maybe the girls are afraid they'll get bitten next!" Janice reached her wriggling fingers toward me as if to imitate a spider, and I pushed her hand away.

"What do you mean, a spider bite?" I questioned. "What're you talking about?" I was going to ask Janice more, but Nyah approached, dripping beads of soapy water on the floor, and I waved her over. "Hey, what's up with the girls? They're so quiet today."

"It's Aunt Lauren," she said. "She told the others when they were marching to the mess hall that Bri was really sick."

"Really?" I asked. "What did she say specifically?"

"She got bit by a big spider last night, you know. Now, we're all scared. We want Bri to be okay, and we want the spiders to go away."

I chewed my lip. "Is there anything else I need to know?"

Nyah opened her mouth, glanced from me to Janice, then back to me. She closed her mouth and shook her head. Without a word, she shuffled off and found a table to wipe down. I turned to Janice.

"What's with her?" I asked.

"I don't know, but didn't I tell you?" Janice asked and crossed her arms. "It was a spider. We've got to get some bug spray."

"Yeah," I said slowly. "Hey, have you seen any spiders lately?"

Janice curled her lip in disgust. "God, no! Can you imagine how the girls would react if they did?"

"I know," I said. "I'm just wondering how Bri

got a spider bite when there aren't any spiders around."

Janice furrowed her eyebrows. "She could be allergic to something in the woods. Maybe she had a reaction last night, and Aunt Lauren took her to the nurse's cabin. Then, she went home. Kinda like that kid who had hay fever a few years ago."

I thought about it. "Yeah, that kid made a lot of noise that year," I said. "Marcus told me the kid woke up several others because he kept wheezing in their bunkhouse."

Janice sucked in a deep breath and raised her eyebrows. "You know, I don't think anyone woke up last night. I didn't, and I'm a light sleeper."

"Hmmm..." I rubbed my chin. "Did any of the girls talk about it this morning?"

"Shoot, you missed it. Aunt Lauren told us on our way to mess hall about the spider bite. It freaked the girls out."

"I think Nyah was freaked out the most." I chewed my lip thoughtfully. "She stiffened up when I asked her about what happened at campfire, too. She brushed me off and rushed out of the bunkhouse. I practically had to run to keep up with her."

"That's weird," Janice said. "She doesn't rush for anything. Except for maybe dessert."

I glanced at the clock. "You can handle the girls

for five minutes, right?"

"Sure, what's up?"

"Not sure," Alissa said. "But I'm gonna catch up with Marcus."

"Oh, really?" Janice asked, coyly. "You two were getting a little cozy at the breakfast line. What's going on there?"

"It's nothing." I suddenly felt a lock tickle my cheek, so I swiped it behind my ear. "We've got to plan for something this afternoon."

Janice shimmied her shoulders and grinned. "All of this sounds so mysterious. You gonna catch me up later?"

"Uh, yeah." My face felt hot. I knew what Janice was getting at. "I'll catch you up later."

I headed out the closest exit. I had to get out of there before I was forced into some awkward conversation about going with a boy I've known since forever. More importantly, I needed to catch up with Marcus. He'd want to hear about the alleged spider bite.

A light jog across the soccer field got me on the path leading through the cluster of bunkhouses nestled beneath the pine trees. Three bunkhouses down from where I was, a door opened and Mr. Roberts, holding a clipboard, exited. I ducked behind a cabin door and saw Mr. Roberts head over to Marcus' and Nate's bunkhouse. The door opened to the wild squeals of boys as they thumped across the planks. As the door was swinging shut, I saw an object hit Mr. Roberts in the face. He yelled, and I waited right where I was.

Chapter 10

Marcus

8:25 a.m.

Fifteen heads swiveled toward the bunkhouse door where Mr. Roberts stood, arm extended, his fingers pinching the elastic band of a pair of wet underwear.

"I'm going to ask you again!" he yelled. "Whose are these?"

No one said anything. I scanned the room, looking for the culprit. Nate held a wet towel he had just snapped at two boys, standing in their swim trunks several feet away from him in a frozen attempt to escape. Another boy, standing next to his bunk, shifted his foot to hide a dirty sock that was not his. Mr. Roberts' eye twitched at the movement.

"Was it yours?" he asked with a scowl.

When the boy shook his head and swallowed hard, Mr. Roberts harrumphed and turned to Nate and me. "What are you two thinking, letting them run around like this? Don't they have someplace to be?"

"Yes," I said, clearing my throat. "We were just—"

"Speak up, Marcus," commanded Mr. Roberts. He stepped toward me. "Why is this place such a mess?"

"They were cleaning up," Nate piped up. "Some kid threw the undies because they weren't his. To be honest, I don't think they belong to anyone."

"Shocking," Mr. Roberts said sarcastically. He stretched out the elastic of the underwear. A couple of kids giggled when this revealed a stain. If Mr. Roberts heard the snickering or noticed the stain, he didn't let on. Instead, his eyes lit up, and he smiled widely at his discovery. He shook out the underwear. "The tag says Dylan. Where's Dylan?"

No one said anything, but the glances of the boys gave the culprit away. A tiny boy with bright red hair shrank in the corner of the room. Mr.

Roberts tossed the pair of underwear to the boy. It landed on the bunkhouse floor.

Bummer, I thought. Dylan left the safety of his little corner to pick it up while everyone watched.

"Mystery solved, boys!" Mr. Roberts exclaimed. "You're all going to clean up this mess." No one moved, and Mr. Roberts clapped his hands several times. "Now!"

The campers scattered. As Nate and I reached for misplaced objects on the floor, Mr. Roberts stopped us. I couldn't imagine what he wanted now.

"I need to talk to you both," he replied.

"We're sorry," I replied. I glanced at Nate, who nodded. "We didn't know they'd make a mess and—"

"It happens," said Mr. Roberts, cutting my apology short with a wave of his hand. "Especially when the senior counselor isn't around. Uncle Craig will join you shortly before he heads up to the archery range. Nate, I need you to oversee all of this." Mr. Roberts made a sweeping gesture with his hand toward the campers scurrying to clean up the mess.

"Marcus, step outside with me," said Mr. Roberts.

I took a deep breath and glanced at Nate, who gave me an I've-got-this-bro-be-cool look. I followed Mr. Roberts out the door. The girls across the path, led by Janice, were filing into their bunkhouse to get changed for swimming. I didn't see Alissa with them.

"Now then," Mr. Roberts said. "Aside from the mess in the bunkhouse, I don't think you'll be any trouble unless you'd like to go home, too." Though I was a few inches taller than Mr. Roberts, I got the feeling he looked down on me. Mr. Roberts licked his lips, waiting for a reply. I blinked and pretended to play dumb.

"Who else went home?" I asked.

"Haven't you heard?" Mr. Roberts asked. "Your sister. She was a real problem last night. She kept the other kids awake with all kinds of noise."

I stiffened. "That's really weird. Bri is never like that at school. Are you sure it was her?"

"Of course, I am!" Mr. Roberts shouted.

I flinched, and Mr. Roberts took notice.

He lowered his voice. "I've been doing this longer than you've been alive. Longer than your parents have been alive, even. This, as you know, is not school. Camp Lenape is not like that public school you all go to where the kids can run rampant. Here we emphasize respect and integrity."

I crossed my arms. I wanted to walk away, but I needed answers. "Where were the warnings, then? You don't just send kids home without any kind of warning."

"We've got to have order here!" Mr. Roberts yelled. The muscles tensed in his neck and his Adam's apple bobbed at his pale throat.

I took a step back. I'd never seen the man like this before. His face turned red.

"Everything here has to be neat and tidy!" Mr. Roberts continued to yell. "Orderly! No one is going to disrespect the camp rules!"

I looked away from Mr. Roberts. He had some insane ways of demonstrating respect to others. I had a mind to tell him that, too, when the door across the path opened. Janice led her campers, dressed in swimwear with towels draped over their shoulders, out of their bunkhouse.

The door behind me opened a crack. A mop of tangled blonde hair appeared. Nate waved and attempted a smile.

"We're ready," Nate said as he swung the door open wider to reveal the campers lined up with their towels over their shoulders.

"Excellent," Mr. Roberts said and stepped past me to inspect the bunkhouse.

Nate shot me a questioning glance. I blew out my cheeks and shrugged in response.

"All right, boys," Mr. Roberts said. "Your room looks amazing. It's like night and day in here. Nate, lead them away."

From the top step, Mr. Roberts looked down on me. Bobbing heads passed between us as the line proceeded out the door. He jutted his chin and smirked as he placed his hands on his hips. I stepped back to allow the campers to pass more quickly. When they'd all gone, Mr. Roberts stepped down and patted me on the shoulder. I sidestepped away from him.

"We're understood then?" Mr. Roberts asked. I gave him a slight nod, and he grinned. "Excellent. Good talk."

Though I'd understood the warning Mr. Roberts gave, I had no idea what he was talking about. I felt as though I knew less than I did before. When Mr. Roberts had gone, I slumped my shoulders and turned to climb the steps into the bunkhouse. I really didn't feel like swimming, but I still had to show up for my duty.

"Hey, Marcus!" called a familiar voice.

I turned. "Hey, Alissa. When did you get here?"

"I heard the whole thing. Mr. Roberts is so wrong!"

"I know. Bri wouldn't act like that. And you would've told me, anyway."

Alissa nodded rapidly. "There's more. According to the girls, even Janice, Aunt Lauren said Bri was sent home because she was bitten by a spider."

I raked my hands through my hair. "That reason makes less sense than the behavior problem Mr. Roberts mentioned. She wouldn't have a reaction to a spider bite. The only poisonous spider around here is a brown recluse, and the bunkhouses are too cool day and night for them to be hanging out there."

Alissa raised her eyebrows. "I don't know about all that. But something is definitely rotten in the state of Denmark."

"Without a doubt. Should we call the police?"

"Maybe we should try calling home first," Alissa offered.

I nodded slowly. "Then if Bri's not there, I'll call the police."

"Sounds like a plan. Let's follow the others." Alissa tapped her foot.

I cocked my head. "Why would we go to the pool?"

Alissa groaned and rolled her eyes. "You're so dense. We're going to the nurse's station. That's the closest phone."

Chapter 11

Alissa

8:38 a.m.

On our way to the nurse's station, I stopped suddenly and grabbed Marcus by the shirt. Nyah was in the pool and sandwiched between two girls.

"Marcus, hold on a sec," I said.

Together, we approached the perimeter fence of the pool and saw Nyah standing waist-deep in the water with two girls, the strawberry-blonde Veronica and her freckle-faced friend Tanya. They were towering over her.

"Leave me alone!" Nyah shouted.

"I bet she didn't say that last night," Veronica said with a sneer.

"Probably not," said Tanya, smirking.

"What the—" Marcus paused as he took in the scene.

"I know," I said. "Be right back, okay?"

With no time to waste, I hopped the fence instead of going through the gated doorway. Casually, I approached the girls from the poolside.

"Hey," I said. "What are you three doing?"

"Nothing," Veronica said curtly. "C'mon, Tanya. Let's go."

Veronica pulled Tanya away, and the two girls swam into the deep end. Nyah, teary-eyed, remained where she stood. A lifeguard and a few of the kids scowled at me.

I ignored them as I crossed my legs and sat at the edge of the pool.

"Nyah, what's wrong?" I asked.

Nyah sniffed. I glanced at Marcus, who was leaning on the fence. His eyes were set on the center of the pool. I followed his gaze. Janice and Nate were there, talking and standing far too close to each other. I blinked a few times. Seeing them together was new to me. I returned my attention to Nyah, who rolled her eyes.

"They've been talking like that since we got

here," she replied. Nyah stuck out her tongue and pretended to gag.

"Oh," I said.

It hadn't occurred to me that Janice would be into Nate. But it made me smile. I decided to change the subject and leaned toward Nyah.

"Can you tell me about those girls?"

Nyah took a deep breath and let out a sigh. "Those two told me someone grabbed Bri last night. They said I should've been grabbed, too."

I tensed. The fence behind us rattled, then Marcus appeared.

"Did you see who took Bri?" he asked as he squatted beside us. "What did they look like?"

"I don't know," Nyah whispered. Her lip trembled.

Marcus and I exchanged a glance. I touched his shoulder to let him know I got this. Then, I turned to Nyah.

"Can you tell us what you do know?" I asked Nyah softly. "Anything can help."

"I really don't know anything," Nyah whimpered. Fresh tears began to form in her eyes. "We were all in the room, and no one saw or heard anything." With that, Nyah dipped her head down and swam away underwater.

A whistle blew. We looked over to the sound. Mr. Roberts was standing on the other side of the pool. His face was bright red.

"Everybody out of the pool!" he yelled.

Janice sank until she was neck-deep in the water. Nate remained standing next to her.

"Nate and Janice," said Mr. Roberts, "you two get out, too."

Nate and Janice seemed to be frozen at a standstill. All eyes were on them.

"What's the holdup?" asked Marcus in a whisper, gently elbowing me.

"I don't know," I whispered, "but look." I pointed to Janice.

Janice rose slowly. She wore a yellow triangle bikini top. I drew in a short, sharp breath.

I'd been with her when she bought the bikini at Forever 21 almost a month ago. I couldn't believe she'd wear it to camp. We all knew the camp rules strictly required girls to wear nothing short of a swim T-shirt. String bikinis of any kind were forbidden. Out of the corner of my eye, I caught Marcus staring. I slapped him lightly in the stomach.

"Ouch," he whispered. He rubbed his stomach in the spot where I hit him. "What was that for?"

I rolled my eyes.

Janice climbed out of the pool, grabbed her swim T-shirt from a bench and shoved a wet arm into a sleeve. Before she could get the other arm in, Mr. Roberts came over to her.

He appeared to whisper something in her ear.

Janice took a step back and nodded. Nate held up a towel for her, and she snatched it out of his hand. Wrapping herself in it, she ran off to the bunkhouse. I followed her.

Chapter 12

Marcus

8:48 a.m.

I stood there in stunned silence as Alissa ran after Janice. Mr. Roberts watched them go for a moment and turned toward the remaining campers. He was about to speak when Nate marched toward him.

"Dude," Nate said to Mr. Roberts. "What's your problem?"

"Shots fired!" shouted one of the boys. The others oohed like they did in school when someone had been called to the office. Mr.

Roberts blew his whistle again.

Mr. Roberts was clearly unprepared to be called out by anyone, let alone a junior camp counselor. To be honest, I was shocked that Nate was going toe-to-toe with him. From where I was standing, Mr. Roberts could've done almost anything. He could've yelled at Janice the way he yelled at me. But Mr. Roberts didn't. He said something to her that no one else, except for Nate, could've possibly heard.

Everyone was silent as they waited for Mr. Roberts to respond to Nate. The only noise came from the gentle bubbling of the pool circulation system. Mr. Roberts cleared his throat.

"There is a dress code that you must follow," he said calmly. He frowned while wagging his finger. "And that is not how you talk to me." He pointed at a group of boys, and then he pointed at Nate. "No one can speak to me rudely. Is that clear?" No one responded, so Mr. Roberts blew his whistle. "Is that clear?"

While the campers nodded in fear, I shook my head at Nate. He must've mistaken it for a nod of approval. He shot me a cocky wink while Mr. Roberts glared at him.

"I'll talk to you in a minute," he told Nate. "Now to the rest of you, get back in the pool. You still have ten..." He glanced at the clock tower. "Oops! You have five minutes before you need to get out and change."

Some did as they were told. Most opted to dry off early and wait until it was time to return to the bunkhouses. Nate stayed in front of Mr. Roberts.

"You," Mr. Roberts seethed. "Who do you think you are, undermining everything this camp stands for?"

Nate peered around at his growing audience. "Who do you think you are, Mr. Roberts?"

Mr. Roberts gave a booming laugh. "Well, I'm the owner of this camp. I'm the one who makes the rules around here, and I'm the one who—"

"Body shames girls."

Geez, Nate, where'd that come from? I thought.

Mr. Roberts was speechless. For a moment, I wondered what he was going to do. I looked between Nate and Mr. Roberts, wondering who would talk first.

"Head up to my house right now and wait on the porch for me," demanded Mr. Roberts.

Nate shrugged. "Should that be before or after I change?"

"Just go!" Mr. Roberts barked.

Nate grabbed his towel and shirt and headed toward the house.

I realized then that I was the only one remaining to escort the kids back to their bunkhouses and supervise them as they got ready for their next activity. I caught up with Mr.

Roberts before he exited the gate.

"Excuse me, sir," I said.

"What?" Mr. Roberts asked sternly as he pivoted on his heel. He stared at me for a moment until his features softened. "I'm sorry, I didn't mean to raise my voice."

I scratched my head, unsure of what to make of Mr. Roberts' behavior. I decided to approach him with caution. "You know, don't you need to radio Uncle Craig since you sent Nate away? I mean, I can escort the campers to the bunkhouses. I'm sure Alissa and Janice will be able to help once we're there."

Mr. Roberts shook his head and gave a forced chuckle. "Don't worry about that. But I'm glad you're here." He pulled a thin envelope out of his pocket and handed it to me.

"What's this?" I flipped the envelope front and back.

"It's a letter from your parents and your sister."

"Why didn't they just call? Or—"

"Phone's dead." Mr. Roberts' face turned grim. "You should read it."

I cracked a knuckle with my free hand. As I slipped my finger in the envelope flap to tear it open, Mr. Roberts cleared his throat. I looked up, and he wagged his finger at me.

"Don't open it now, my boy," he said. "Open it later." Mr. Roberts patted me on my shoulder as he walked past and started to whistle an off-key tune.

With the envelope clenched in my fist, I led the campers, boys and girls, back to the bunkhouses. As I rounded the corner of the first bunkhouse, I stopped short, and the campers ran past me.

Aunt Lauren was facing Alissa and Janice. Both girls were frowning. Janice was turned slightly away from Aunt Lauren. They looked up as their campers rushed toward their bunkhouses.

"Hey, girls," Alissa called cheerfully. "How was the rest of your swim?"

Janice weakly high-fived a couple of girls as they passed. Understandably, she lacked Alissa's enthusiasm. Aunt Lauren touched Janice lightly on the shoulder and approached me.

"Hey, Marcus, thanks for taking over at the end," she said. "Keep up the good work, okay?"

"Sure," I said. "Can you tell me what happened to Bri?"

Aunt Lauren avoided eye contact. "Didn't you hear? Mr. Roberts should've told you already."

I nodded. "Yeah, he did. I just wanted to hear it from you. You were in the cabin after all. I wanted to know exactly how it all went down."

"No problem." Aunt Lauren paused.

Then, she leaned toward me. For a reason I couldn't quite place, her gesture felt wrong, so I took a step back.

"Bri complained of a tummy ache," Aunt Lauren continued. "I checked her forehead to see if she had a—"

"I thought she was bitten by a spider," I interrupted.

Aunt Lauren's breath hitched. "She...was. So, it sounds like you know everything. I'm sure she's resting. I've got to head over to arts and crafts. I'll see you there later." Aunt Lauren hurried off without another word. I watched her leave before heading over to Alissa and Janice.

"What was that about?" asked Alissa.

"More of the same," I said. "Aunt Lauren just confirmed what you already told me about Bri. Only, she began with a line about a tummy ache until I interrupted her with the spider bite."

Alissa frowned. "That doesn't make any sense."

"I know. Seems some of the adults around here can't keep their stories straight. And Mr. Roberts gave me this." I held up the envelope and told her what it contained.

"This place is really starting to suck," Janice chimed in. "I've got to go see Mr. Roberts at his house." She pointed to my envelope. "You going to open that, or what?"

"Yeah," I sighed as I slipped the pages out. There were two letters. I read aloud the first one from Bri:

Marcus,

Last night I made a lot of noise in the cabin. I couldn't sleep. That's why Mr. Roberts and the night guard came and got me. Mom and Dad were already waiting at the parking lot. I'm sorry.

Bri

"What the heck," Alissa and Janice said in unison.

"Why would she write this if she was sick?" I questioned. I swallowed hard, and my hands trembled.

"Here," said Alissa, "let me read the next one." She took the other letter from my shaky hands and started reading:

Marcus,

We are disappointed in Bri's behavior. She's home now and will be punished accordingly. We expect you to continue as you always do by being respectful and actively leading your cabin in upholding Camp Lenape's code of conduct.

Mom and Dad

"This doesn't sound anything like your parents," Alissa said, handing the letter back to me. "And the first one definitely doesn't sound like your sister."

"She wouldn't apologize for anything," I said through clenched teeth. "I'm no expert, but something about the handwriting is off. I mean, the letter looks like Bri wrote it. But the one from my parents reminds me of the time in middle school when I made up a sick note by tracing my mom's signature."

"I remember that," Alissa said somberly. "You were grounded forever when they found out."

"Okay, guys," Janice said. "This is all really intriguing. I've got to head out before I'm in deeper trouble. Whatever you do, let me know, okay?"

"Absolutely," Alissa said as she and Janice hugged. "Good luck up there."

Janice breathed in deep and raised her eyebrows. She looked like she wanted to say something more. She exhaled, then turned and jogged off toward the house.

"So," Alissa said. "What's the plan? I vote we call the police."

I shook my head. "Can't. Mr. Roberts said the phone is down."

"Crap, that means we can't go to the nurse's station and use the phone like we had planned." Alissa kicked the dirt. "Wish we could just use our cell phones."

I glanced around and pulled out my own and held it up. "No service right here."

Alissa's mouth flew open as she swatted at me. "Put your phone away before someone sees it. There's a call box two miles north of the camp. I could run there and—"

"What's a call box?" I asked.

She shook her head. "Seriously?"

The girls' bunkhouse door popped open, and Alissa's campers started to line up.

"Short explanation," Alissa said, "my dad says they used to be all over the freeways."

I looked at my own bunkhouse. A crash from inside told me the boys were getting a little rowdy.

"I need to get my guys together," I said. "So, when we go to this call box, we'll phone the police, and this is all over?"

"Something like that," Alissa said. "Why don't you get your guys to archery. Aunt Lauren will be on me big time if I'm late for arts and crafts. Try to sneak off through the cornfields when Nate catches up with you. We need to get on this real quick."

"All right, girls, let's go!" Alissa shouted to her campers.

I opened my bunkhouse door, and my campers piled out. If Mr. Roberts were around, he'd have a fit. But he wasn't around, and I wouldn't have cared anyway.

"Be careful," Alissa said as she passed me.

That was the plan, although I needed to figure

out how to sneak away as soon as Nate arrived at
archery.

Chapter 13

Alissa

9:36 a.m.

I sat with my girls in the arts-and-crafts pavilion. A warm, humid breeze flowed through and threatened a storm.

In the front of the pavilion, Aunt Lauren flashed examples of trinkets that the girls would learn how to thread into friendship bracelets. Some of the girls oohed at the way they sparkled when they caught the sunlight. Once Aunt Lauren started her demonstration, the girls were hooked. Aunt Lauren called for an assistant. Five girls elbowed each other as they fought to be her first helper.

"How about you?" Aunt Lauren pointed out freckle-faced girl, Tanya.

The other four girls sulked but forgot about not being picked the moment the demonstration began. They clearly liked threading sequins and gold or silver plastic chains into bracelets. I, on the other hand, was bored.

I had seen Aunt Lauren's demonstration many times over the years, so it wasn't new. Last year, I even wove a friendship bracelet into one of my braids. I zoned out, looking down the pathway and hoping Janice would appear. She had been gone for a while, and I was growing anxious. Janice chose today to wear the bikini, and it just so happened Mr. Roberts did see her. I wondered what her punishment would be. I began running a mental list of possibilities: doing a public apology, no swimming for a week, or maybe wearing an old, camp-provided bathing suit.

"Alissa!" Aunt Lauren shouted, snapping me out of my thoughts. "Thanks for joining us again." She had a twinge of irritation in her voice. "I was saying you can work with this half of the group over here, and I'll guide this half over here. When Janice gets here, she can take my place, and I will bounce between the groups. Got it?"

"Yes, ma'am," I said obediently.

I went to my assigned group, but I wasn't into

the activity. If I were a camper, I probably would have wanted to make a bracelet. I would even have marveled at the cool, new materials being used. Still, I had to pretend I was enjoying the process or else Aunt Lauren would call me out again.

I began working with one smaller girl, who was a bit clumsy with the string. Her teary little voice made my heart melt as she pointed to the example, showing me beads she wanted to include. She kept tying ugly knots instead of threading the bracelet into cute little waves or chevrons. I figured she was trying to make one with chevrons, so I proceeded to undo the knots she made. After a while, I started to enjoy myself, and the little girl's tears dried up as her friendship bracelet started to look better.

"Hey, gimme that back!" someone shouted from the other side of the pavilion. It was Nyah, fighting over some beads and thread with the girls Veronica and Tanya from the pool. Before things could get violent, Janice slid into the pavilion and stopped the fight.

"There's plenty to go around," she said. She guided Veronica and Tanya to another table. "Here, let's figure this out."

Janice had seemed to pop out of nowhere. I must have been so engaged in making the dumb bracelets that I hadn't noticed her arrival. She found a table and began to help the girls.

"Nyah, why don't you bring your materials over to this table?" Aunt Lauren asked from across the pavilion.

Nyah became wide-eyed. Her brown eyes glistened, and they looked like they were pleading to me for help. Sadly, I could only defer to Aunt Lauren's authority.

"It's okay, Nyah," I said. "Aunt Lauren will help you. You're not in trouble."

Nyah nodded slowly, and I could tell she didn't believe me. I didn't believe me either. Bri was the last girl I sent to Aunt Lauren, and she disappeared. Also, Aunt Lauren could be intense, though she patiently sat at her table, waiting for Nyah. A couple of girls already sitting with Aunt Lauren glared at Nyah, but Aunt Lauren didn't notice. She waved some pretty friendship bracelets in her hand to coax Nyah to come over.

"Go ahead, Nyah," I said. "She won't bite." But she might tell lies about you, I mentally added.

Nyah rolled her eyes and headed to the material table. She filled her hands with the beads and a bracelet she had started, then slowly walked to Aunt Lauren. I felt bad for her, but there wasn't anything I could do now. I continued working with the girls in my group. Janice walked over to assist me.

"When did you get here?" I asked her.

"I was coming up the path when I saw them fighting," Janice said. "So, I ran the rest of the way and got between them." Janice lowered her voice. "Is Nyah okay?"

"No," I whispered back. "Those girls you moved away—"

"Alissa and Janice, please focus on the campers," interrupted Aunt Lauren. She stood up from her table. "Save social hour for your break." Aunt Lauren returned to her seat.

With Aunt Lauren preoccupied, I decided now was a good time to talk to Veronica and Tanya, especially since this was the second time this morning they had picked on Nyah. As I approached their table, they were laughing, but their expressions turned stony as soon as they saw me.

"Oh, girls," I sang sweetly. "I think it's time to talk. Don't you agree?"

"We don't want to talk to you," replied Veronica. She was snotty, and I thought she was acting too grown-up for her age.

"Are you sure you don't want to talk to me?" I asked them.

"Yup," said Veronica.

I'm really beginning to dislike this kid, I thought. Still, I needed information from her.

"Well," I said, leaning in close, "you can talk to me, Aunt Lauren, or worse...Mr. Roberts."

With narrowed eyes, the girls glanced at each other before Veronica spoke.

"Look," she said. "Nyah is nosy. We just don't want her around."

"Tell me," I demanded. Veronica and Tanya didn't respond, so I tried a different approach. I worked a knot of my friendship bracelet, keeping my eyes focused on the girls. Really, I could have made this bracelet in my sleep, but they didn't know that. I effortlessly worked the embroidery floss, and the two girls were silent, enamored by my work.

"How'd you do that?" asked Tanya. Her bright, blue eyes followed my hands manipulating the embroidery floss into little knots. I carefully wove the floss around the bracelet.

"Oh, you mean this?" I looked at the bracelet I was making and shrugged like it was no big deal. "I could teach you."

"Really?" asked Veronica.

"But, first..." I stopped threading the floss and looked each of them in the eye. "You two have got to tell me what's going on between you and Nyah. Whatever it is has to stop."

The two girls fidgeted in their seats and contemplated what to do. I imagined them weighing their options: keep their secret or make the most fashionable camp bracelet they had ever seen. They frowned. They shared a glance, and then they told me everything they knew.

"Bri said there was this man in the woods," said Veronica. "She almost ran into him when she went to the bathroom last night."

I brushed a braid back behind my ear. I had heard as much already. Nyah, unfortunately, hadn't said anything at all. So, I braced myself for the worst. I hoped one of these two girls knew something.

"Then last night, we saw a man come into our cabin," Tanya whispered. "He covered Bri's mouth."

"Yeah," agreed Veronica. "She didn't struggle, either. He picked her right up. Then, this woman suddenly appeared in the room and—"

"What do you mean by suddenly?" I asked, trying to hold back my shock. Veronica made it sound as if the woman had teleported in there. I couldn't tell whether these girls were being honest or stretching the truth.

"You couldn't see her at first," Tanya said. "But she was in the room, and suddenly we could see her."

I glanced up at Aunt Lauren, who flashed me a how's-it-going-over-there smile. I smiled and waved her away. She was hiding something. I just needed to know what.

"Tell me more about this woman," I whispered to the girls. "Where'd she come from?"

"She came from the shadows," replied Veronica, blinking rapidly.

"Then," said Tanya, "she held the door open as the man left the room."

I was stunned. The scenario the two girls described sounded like something out of a scary movie. I worried about Bri's safety.

"Did you recognize any of them?" I asked.

"Just the woman," Veronica said. "It was Aunt Lauren."

My skin crawled. Aunt Lauren had told a story about a spider bite that didn't jive with Mr. Roberts' story about Bri being in trouble. The girls' account of last night suggested that Aunt Lauren was helping these kidnappers. I needed more. I was thirsty for information.

"Did they say anything to Bri that you could hear?"

Both girls shook their heads. I realized I was freaking them out, so I tried to put them at ease.

"How would you like to learn how to weave a friendship bracelet into your hair?"

"Yeah!" they chimed in unison. Their faces beamed. Veronica was almost adorable.

"Cool," I said. "I need you to do one more thing for me."

"What's that?" Tanya asked.

I paused. "Why are you picking on Nyah?"

"Oh, that," Veronica said and rolled her eyes as

she turned away. She spoke to Tanya. "You tell her."

Tanya spoke. "Bri was the only girl Nyah hung out with and now that Bri is gone, she wants to hang out with us."

"But we don't want her around," Veronica finished.

"Why not?" I asked.

Veronica scrunched her face. "If you need to know, it's because she likes Henrick in Cabin Seven. Henrick is my boyfriend, and no one else can have him."

Geez, little girl drama, I thought.

"Well, please be nice to Nyah," I said. "I promise that I'll meet with you during our free time and pass on my bracelet-making skills, okay?"

"Okay," the girls said in unison.

I needed to get to Marcus right away. He needed to hear about what happened to his sister, especially since, I realized, he had literally witnessed her kidnapping last night.

As I wandered to the next group of girls, Janice tugged my arm.

"Were Veronica and Tanya nice?" she asked jokingly.

"As a matter of fact, they were," I said. "They told me everything I needed to know."

Janice gave me a confused look.

"Let me explain." As I filled her in, Janice

gasped and covered her mouth with her hand.

"You've got to call the police," she said.

I cringed. "Hopefully Marcus is headed out now to a call box. The phone at camp is down."

Janice shook her head. "It isn't. When we were there, Mr. Roberts received a call. We heard the phone ring."

"Alissa and Janice," Aunt Lauren called to us. She stood up. "Stop standing around. Your campers need help."

"I'm sorry, Aunt Lauren," I replied. "I've got to go."

I was gone before Aunt Lauren could say anything. I knew Janice would cover for me.

Chapter 14

Marcus

9:55 a.m.

Nate and I stole into a thicket just behind the Roberts house. I crouched behind a tree, while Nate stood behind another tree to scope out the house. From my position, I could see everything behind us.

"All right." Nate joined me behind the tree. "Roberts is headed out for rounds."

"What about his wife?" I asked. "What if she goes inside?"

"Nah," Nate said. "That glass she was drinking

on the front porch was still very full."

"I know, but still...it seems risky."

Nate looked at me. "Don't worry, okay? I've been here before. We'll go through the basement, which leads up to the kitchen. The phone is right there next to the steps. There's no way Mrs. Roberts will catch us."

Somehow Nate had managed to explore the Roberts house while he and Janice were supposed to be writing an apology letter to be read to the camp during lunch. Though I didn't understand Nate's methods, I knew they were effective. Besides, I had more important things to worry about. As soon as Nate met me at archery and told me the phone worked in their house, we were gone without a word to Uncle Craig, our archery instructor. He could handle the end of the activity period himself. Our campers would wait until they had an escort to arts and crafts before heading off. I knew Alissa and Janice would pick up the slack. I was counting on Alissa to understand that the plans had changed slightly.

"You ready?" Nate asked.

"Race you there," I said.

We took off. The clearing between the woods and the house didn't provide much cover. There was no way for us to know whether Mrs. Roberts would go inside and see us from a window. We stopped when we reached the basement door.

"Hey, won't it be locked?" I asked.

"Probably," Nate said as he shrugged. That's why I have this." He pulled out a pick kit.

"Why would you bring that to camp with you?"

Nate gave me a thumbs-up. "You need to be prepared for everything. I brought my Leatherman, too."

"Oh, so I guess I should have been prepared for my sister mysteriously disappearing, too?" I rolled my eyes. "Did you bring a satellite phone with you as well? That'd come in handy."

Nate bit his lip as he jimmied the keyhole. "I haven't gotten one yet. But I'm saving up. Maybe next year."

My expression softened. "Sorry, bro. I didn't mean to talk to you like that. I'm just a little on edge about Bri."

Nate nodded. "Dude, it's okay. I want to find your sister as much as you do."

After a few more tries, Nate popped the lock open. We were inside, and we closed the door behind us. Just as my eyes began to adjust to the darkness, Nate switched on a flashlight.

"What'd you do?" I asked. "Go back to the bunkhouse and get your gear?"

He shook his head. "There's a reason I wear cargo shorts all of the time."

Nate had always seemed to be prepared for just about anything during our past adventures. I wanted to believe that this time was no different, but this operation was definitely impromptu. There was no way he could've planned this out. We weren't on a pretend secret mission now.

Nate scanned his flashlight through the basement. It was unfinished, with concrete floors. We were standing in a hallway that cornered out ten feet in front of us. To our left was a concrete wall that was damp to the touch. To our right was an unpainted sheetrock wall with a door. Nate grabbed it, turned the handle down, and popped the door open.

"What are you doing?" I asked in a hushed tone. As much as I wanted to yell at him, I knew that wouldn't do any good in our current predicament.

Nate motioned me to follow him. I stepped through the door, and the light flicked on.

Nate whistled softly. "Check this place out."

It was a finished office space with the kind of thin, cheap carpeting you might find in the front office of a school. On a steel desk sat a monitor that flashed various images: a bunkhouse, the pool, the front entrance, a pathway. We were watching CCTV. Nate voiced the question on my mind.

"Why would Mr. Roberts need all of these cameras for a camp?" he asked.

I was still fixated on the monitor when a rundown cottage flashed on the screen.

"Check that out," I said. "Isn't that the cottage our counselors told us about in the old ghost story?"

"Yeah," Nate said. "It was the house Mr. Roberts grew up in or something."

According to camp lore, Mr. Roberts' father had died of a heart attack in the cottage while trying to renovate it. No one, except for some mischievous campers, like Nate and me, had been in it ever since. Two summers ago, we'd snuck over to the cottage. We'd been thoroughly disappointed that it was nothing but a rundown old house.

"Stuff to scare the kids at night," I said. Then a map by the monitors caught my attention. "Look at this." I picked it up.

Nate came over. The map showed all ten acres of what I knew to be Camp Lenape. Beyond the camp, someone had circled a plot of land almost four miles away.

"What's with the circle?" I asked.

"It's where the old cottage is located," Nate said. "See here." He pointed to the northeastern corner of the camp. "That's where the pathway begins. There's even a trail marked on the map, leading to the cottage."

I followed his index finger along a dotted line that snaked through the forest surrounding the camp. The pathway led to a small clearing where the cottage was located.

"Does Mr. Roberts own all this?" I asked.

"I don't think so," Nate said. "The forest is probably government land."

Nate stepped away from me and pulled open a drawer. I spotted a phone on the table behind Nate and picked up the receiver. I nearly gasped when I heard talking on the line.

A female voice said, "Is she all right? I need to know."

Then a man said, "How'd you get this number? Your husband—"

The woman—it had to be Mrs. Roberts—interrupted him. "For God's sake, you know who runs this show!"

There was a pause. I felt my heart beating rapidly against my rib cage. I held my hand against the receiver's mouth and hoped they couldn't hear me. Nate was staring; I held up my other hand for him to keep quiet.

The man said, "But we dealt with your husband."

Mrs. Roberts responded, "If the girl's harmed—"

Then he said, "Is someone else with you?"

I held my breath.

"No, why would—"

"Someone else is with you," he insisted. "Just keep your end of the deal. We'll be out by tomorrow night. The girl will be here waiting."

There was a click.

Mrs. Roberts said, "Hello, is anyone there?"

Was she speaking to me? I thought. Nate and I had tried to be as quiet as possible, but maybe they'd heard us breathing.

"Tom, is that you?"

I didn't answer. The phone clicked. I placed the receiver down.

"We've got to get out of here," I said.

"Hold on a sec," Nate answered.

The floor above us creaked. Nate looked up. He grabbed a file folder that he'd been scanning.

"Okay, let's go," Nate said. I flicked off the light switch almost at the same time he turned on his flashlight. "Follow me."

The basement lights turned on. Nate and I froze.

"Tom, are you down there?" Mrs. Roberts was calling to her husband.

I didn't know what they were up to, but I hoped whatever was in the file Nate held would give us some answers.

"I hope it's not some junior counselors," Mrs. Roberts' voice came again. "Because I've got a loaded shotgun and I'd hate to kill you."

Another creak and I realized she was beginning to descend the steps. We didn't need another warning. We bolted and didn't even bother to shut the door behind us.

Chapter 15

Alissa

10:05 a.m.

I clutched a black receiver in my hand. I'd never been this close to a call box before and was staring at the keypad and its red and green buttons. I was still out of breath. I had thought I'd catch up with Marcus at archery, but Uncle Craig told me he and Nate had left in a hurry. That's when I decided to follow the cornfields past the security booth and through the woods. I figured I'd run into them here, but there was no sign of them.

I brushed back a braid, breathed in, and

punched the zero. That usually got an operator. The phone rang.

"Highway patrol," a woman's voice came. "This is Carlotta. What's your emergency?"

"I...uh..." I stuttered. I held my breath, not sure what to say.

"If this is a prank call, I have—"

"No," I squeaked. "I'm sorry. This is...ummm...Alissa. Alissa Claude."

"Hello, Alissa," Carlotta said. "You sound young. Is your Mom or Dad okay?"

"No," I said. "I mean, yes, but I'm not with them. I'm...alone at..." I looked around. "Mile 105."

"Okay, Mile 105 is near Camp Lenape."

I let out a long breath and smiled. "Yes, I'm a junior counselor there, and one of our campers has gone missing and—"

"Hold on a second," Carlotta interrupted. "Why isn't your camp director calling 9-1-1?"

I didn't have an answer. Carlotta probably still thought this was a prank.

"Ms. Carlotta," I said. "Believe me. I wish this were a joke, but it's not."

I began to tell her everything I knew about the man Bri saw in the woods. I was about to explain how a man, helped by Aunt Lauren, took Bri from the bunkhouse last night, when sirens whooped and blue and red lights flashed behind me.

"Wait," I said. "Police are already here."

I set the receiver down, ignoring the buzz of Carlotta's voice on the other end. I didn't need her anymore. The passenger-side window of the cruiser rolled down. A man with dark hair and a baby face smiled at me.

"You okay?" the man asked. "I'm Officer Rogers. Are you lost?"

I shook my head. I approached the vehicle, but stopped when the driver, a tall, bald man, got out and circled around the front of the car. His hand was on the handle of his gun.

My heart felt as if it stopped in my chest. I took several steps back and wished for the comforting voice of Carlotta, who sounded so much like my mother. She would understand. These officers didn't look like me, and I doubted they would treat me fairly as a person of color. I didn't know what the hell I was thinking—me calling the police by myself.

The bald man paused and released his grip on his gun.

"I'm sorry, miss," he said. "I didn't mean to alarm you."

I stared at him. He seemed to be forcing his facial features to soften, though his arms and shoulders still seemed ready to launch into action if needed.

"I'm Officer Duvall," he said. Then he pointed

to the man in the cop car. "This here's Officer Rogers. We got a call about someone missing from camp."

"On our radio," Officer Rogers added from his seat in the car, holding up a small wired speaker. "We were in the area, so we responded. Talk to Duvall here."

"Okay," I said with hesitation.

I looked from Officer Rogers to Duvall, then back to Officer Rogers. He grinned at me with boyish dimples. Duvall, on the other hand, still seemed forced and stiff.

"Alissa," Duvall said quietly. "We're police officers. We're here to help."

I froze. I hadn't given him my name at all. I also couldn't believe that Carlotta would've had time to contact their precinct and send a patrol car out. I had literally just talked to her. I backed away, uncertain of these two. Duvall stepped toward me and reached for something at his belt.

"Steady now," Officer Rogers said calmly. "Don't want to spook the girl."

Too late for that, I thought. I was already spooked. I turned and crashed through brush and branches back toward camp in hopes that the two men wouldn't beat me there.

Dashing through the woods, I knew I had to get away from these guys. Other than their knowing my name, something about the officers seemed off. I felt as though I was being hunted, or maybe even targeted, as though they'd known I would be there at the call box. I just didn't know how that was possible.

As I ran, I kept an ear to the road thirty yards to my right. I took comfort in knowing the treeline would hide my progress, and that I would hear anyone following me. I stopped a few times to listen. Silence prompted me to keep going.

I held my hands up and pushed through some low-hanging branches, a mix of pine and maple. I was going at a good pace when someone smacked directly into me and grabbed me. I felt myself falling forward and screamed.

"Alissa, it's me," said a familiar voice.

I stepped back, and Marcus released me from his embrace. We stood there a moment, each of us surprised to see the other. I noticed a glint in his hazel eyes and a folder in his hand. He had something to tell me. I had something to tell him. But we didn't have time. I grabbed his hand and began to move.

"Hey, we've gotta go," I said.

"What's going on?" Marcus asked.

I stopped and let go of his hand. "Seriously, Marcus, let's go. We're safer back at the camp."

"Did you get a hold of the police?"

I nodded. "Yes, but I don't think they're the real

police."

I didn't have time to explain. Just then, flashing lights caused both of our heads to snap in the same direction.

"C'mon!" I shouted.

I was already running. Marcus had no choice but to follow. We'd have plenty of time to share what we had each discovered. Right now, we had to get as far away from Rogers and Duvall as possible. I only hoped they wouldn't cut us off at the entrance to camp.

Chapter 16

Marcus

10:15 a.m.

Alissa and I ran through the woods. I could already see the camp driveway. Just beyond the road, I could see the rows of cornstalks, their tops rustling roughly beneath a heavy breeze. Rain was in the air.

She didn't know about the folder I was carrying. To be honest, I didn't really understand what it was either, but Nate had shoved it in my hands and told me to get to the police while he figured out our next move. We'll convene on the baseball field at eleven o'clock this morning. Those were his exact words.

"Stop!" I shouted.

Alissa slowed down, so I could catch up. We'd made it almost to the camp entrance.

"What's the matter?" Alissa asked. "Can't keep up?"

"I can," I said between breaths. "But I've got things to share. We need to—"

"So do I," Alissa said. "I know a place we can talk in secret."

She cut hard to the left and disappeared into a bush. I followed her and found myself in a clearing no more than five feet wide and surrounded by a hedge of bushes. Alissa and I were standing incredibly close to each other. So close, I could smell the scent of her coconut-vanilla body spray. Her breathing sounded heavy, and I hoped I'd remembered to put on my deodorant.

"Okay," Alissa rasped. "You go first."

"We found this," I replied. I held up the folder and handed it to Alissa.

Alissa whistled as she thumbed through the contents. "Camp Lenape shouldn't even be in business. Look at this." She held up a report, showing the camp was hundreds of thousands of dollars in debt over the years.

"Flip the page," I said. Nate and I hadn't had a

lot of time to look at the report before we went our separate ways, but he had told me to look at this month's numbers. Alissa flipped the page, and her eyes went wide.

"How'd they get this much money this quickly?" she asked. "Three of the bunkhouses aren't even filled."

"I know. And there's more." I told her about what I'd overheard on the phone.

Alissa waited, nodding rapidly until I finished talking. "You remember Veronica and Tanya, right? They told me a man came in last night and took Bri. The man slung her right over his shoulder."

My heart was racing. Alissa didn't need to finish. I realized Nate and I had witnessed Bri's kidnapping. "How could we've been so stupid? We watched the whole thing." I collapsed, trying to breathe, but only tears came.

"Hey," Alissa whispered as she knelt and pulled me into an embrace. "There's no way you could've known that." Her voice was cracking, too. "He stole her just feet away from me, and Aunt Lauren helped."

I huffed. "She did what?" My mind started spiraling. Alissa stood. I let her take my hand and help me up.

"C'mon," she said. "We've got plans to make if we're going to help Bri."

I followed her. Up to now, Nate had been incredibly resourceful. I'd even consider him meticulous in his planning. But we had no idea what we would be facing.

PART TWO

Chapter 17

Thursday, July 19. 2:00 a.m.

Filled with an uncertainty that threatened their resolve, the four friends trekked quietly along a narrow path that sloped downward. Each of them wore a rain jacket beaded with water. While the dense foliage above protected them from most of the rainfall, they still had to proceed with caution over a surface that became increasingly slick and muddy as they inched their way toward their destination.

The process of elimination had caused Marcus, Alissa, Nate, and Janice to determine that Bri could only be in one place—the cottage in the woods. Indeed, they'd been told it had been torn down just before the start of summer camp. Yet, as Marcus brought up the rear, he recalled with a stabbing pain to his chest the words of Mrs. Roberts: If the girl's harmed...

They'd met over an hour ago at the little clearing adjacent to right field just inside of the woods. Nate reviewed the plan with everyone.

"These guys will probably be awake, clearing out their stuff," he said. "We don't know what that is, but the rain will slow them down. Marcus and I will go in while you two—"

"Excuse me," Alissa interjected with crossed arms and a jaunty tilt of her shoulders. "I am not going to hang out and keep watch. I'm going in."

Marcus glanced at Nate. He knew Nate liked his plans to be followed perfectly. Just as Nate was about to argue with Alissa, Janice stepped close to him.

"I'm okay with keeping watch, Nate," she replied as she wrapped her arm around his waist. "Let them go, and you could stay with me."

Nate flinched. With a clenched jaw, he forced a gust of air through his nostrils.

"Fine," Nate conceded. "But you and Marcus gotta follow the plan perfectly. Go through the back door and head down the steps into the basement."

"Ummm...cabins don't have basements," said

Janice, cocking her head.

"It's not really a cabin," Nate said. "It's more of a cottage." Nate redirected his attention to Marcus and Alissa. "You two should be fine, so long as Marcus avoids floorboards."

"Yeah," said Marcus as he rubbed the back of his neck. "We'll be in the basement, so I'll be fine."

"All this basement talk," Alissa said. "How do we even know Bri's in there?"

A lump large enough to be felt by the other three formed in Marcus' throat. He feared that the most—they might go through all this trouble and find out that she wasn't even there. Nate nodded in solemn agreement with Alissa.

"The truth is we don't know," said Nate quietly. "But that's our best bet. We can't trust the local police, and we can't call out because our cell phones don't get reception. So we're on our own."

Keeping low to the ground, his eyes focused on avoiding muddy holes, Marcus replayed images in his mind, depicting the worst possible scenarios. Suddenly, he bumped into Alissa.

"Good thing we aren't dance partners at the camp luau," Alissa said, turning to him with a smile. "You okay there?"

"Yeah, I'm fine," Marcus said as he shook his head to clear his thoughts. "Why're we stopped?"

Alissa pointed up ahead. Marcus could see the

shadowy form of a roof. He could hear a bubbling creek, overflowing with rainwater.

"You guys take the lead from here," said Nate. "There's a bridge ahead that gets slippery when wet."

"You ready to get your sister, Marcus?" Alissa asked.

Nodding, Marcus stepped forward and clicked on a flashlight he'd been carrying in his back pocket. The rocky slope they'd been navigating opened to a worn stretch of soggy grass and mud. Here, one could look up and see the stars if the sky weren't dark with clouds. Marcus trained his flashlight on a rickety footbridge that connected to the clearing. The light bounced and glistened off puddles of water. He focused his beam farther ahead. Several hundred yards beyond, he could just make out the gabled roof of the cottage. Nate knocked down Marcus' hand.

"Do you want to get caught, or something?" Nate asked.

"Sorry," Marcus mumbled. "I was just..."

"S'okay," Alissa picked up where Marcus' voice trailed off. "I doubt anyone would've seen it if there is even anyone inside."

"Hey," Janice said. "The water's soaking through my jacket. So, if you guys can get this over with, we'll be right here."

"Be careful on the bridge, you two," said Nate.

He nudged Marcus forward. "We'll be right behind you."

Placing a steady foot upon the first rain-soaked board of the bridge, Marcus could feel his heart pounding in his chest. Something about this seemed off, but he'd led his friends this far, and he wouldn't turn back now.

One by one, they crossed the fifteen-foot span of the bridge. Marcus half expected a troll to pop out of the creek and demand payment or try to eat one of them for a midnight snack. The bridge rattled and squeaked but showed no signs of breaking. Once they were across, the pathway sloped slightly, and they descended a set of mossy stone steps until they could see through the trees. The cottage was bordered by cracked pavement that weeds had long since overtaken and claimed as their own. The cottage itself was equally cracked, and saplings even grew from the gutters.

"Do you think anyone lives here?" Janice asked.

"No," Nate and Marcus said simultaneously.

Suddenly, as if to counter their reply, a light from the front of the cottage flickered on.

"Uh," Alissa whispered. "We might have a problem."

Marcus killed his flashlight and stuck it in his back pocket.

"Well, that was definitely unexpected," he said. "What now?"

"Looks like most of the activity is in the front," said Nate as he eyed the cottage. "I counted the shadows of two men."

"And how do you know they're men?" Alissa asked.

Nate shrugged. "Just a guess. Doesn't matter. Still, at least two people are inside."

Marcus pulled out his cell phone. Still no signal. "Guess it's now or never?"

"I'll follow your lead," Alissa said.

Marcus took a step forward, but Nate grabbed him by the shoulder.

"Here, you might need this."

Nate held out his Leatherman multitool. Marcus wasn't entirely sure what he would do with it, but he took it and stuffed it in his empty front pocket. He waved to Janice and Nate before he and Alissa headed down.

Marcus descended the steps, and Alissa followed him. Where the treeline met the drive, he crouched down and was relieved when Alissa did the same. She reacted to the situation like a pro, even though she'd never accompanied Marcus and Nate on the boys' adventures.

Taking one slow step after another, Marcus and Alissa made their way toward the back of the cottage. As they got close, they occasionally paused, half expecting a motion light to pop on. When none did, they picked up their speed. By the time they made it to the back door, they had found themselves in an upright position. Marcus pulled out his flashlight, held one hand over the bulb, and turned it on. The outline of his hand seemed to glow as he and Alissa examined the entrance.

There were double doors. The first still had bits of screen that flaked off to the touch. Marcus gave Alissa a nod when she motioned to the door handle. It opened without a problem. The second door was solid wood with a doorknob that was green with age.

Alissa reached for the knob, and Marcus held his breath, hoping that it would open without a problem. The knob jiggled, then stopped when Alissa turned it. She pushed at the door but found it was stuck.

"I'm pretty sure it'll open," Alissa whispered. "But maybe we can push against it at the same time."

Marcus turned his flashlight off and stuffed it into his back pocket. Alissa shifted close to the edge of the door as Marcus eased in beside her. From his position against the door, a waft of coconut and vanilla mixed with the rot of moldy wood filled his nostrils. He focused on the scent of Alissa's body spray as she counted.

On three, they applied pressure against the door. It squeaked forward but didn't open.

"Let's try again, but put more pressure on the

door this time," Alissa whispered.

They counted again. On three, Marcus and Alissa found themselves flying through the doorway. They landed beside each other, and a light flickered on.

As he started to rise, Marcus realized he was at the foot of a booted individual.

"Well," said the stranger in a deep voice. "Looks like we've got a couple more kids."

Marcus locked eyes with the man, who grinned at him. He was well dressed, with a neatly trimmed beard. Suddenly, Marcus felt a burst of pain in the back of his head. As he crumpled to the floor, he could faintly hear Alissa yelling for him to run, but it was too late.

Chapter 18

Alissa

I jolted awake and found myself sitting upright on a cold, concrete floor. I was in a dark room. A single window in the top corner of one wall told me the time: half past it's-too-dark-to-tell.

Next to me was Marcus. Somehow, between getting knocked on the head and placed in this dungeon, I'd lost my shoes and my raincoat. I glanced toward Marcus, hoping that he'd wake up. They'd taken his shoes and coat, too. Still damp from our walk through the rain, I shivered even though I wasn't cold.

I shook Marcus, but he didn't respond. I guessed he'd been clobbered but good. Before I was knocked on the head, I only caught a glimpse of the man: a trim beard, cold blue eyes, and a man bun. I hated the hipster look. My head throbbed. Dizzily, I stood up and breathed in the musty air. The smell of urine and rotting wood made me gag.

"Alissa," a teary voice that I recognized came from the other side of the room.

"Bri, is that you?"

She was in my arms before I could go to her.

"I'm so happy to see you!" Bri glanced at Marcus. "Is Marcus going to be okay?"

I nodded. "He will be." I broke our hug and looked at her. "Thank God you're okay. Did they hurt you?"

"No, I just want to go home."

"Me too. Let's find a way out."

I looked to the single window in the corner of the room. The window was far too small for me, but maybe Bri would be able to fit through it.

"Don't bother," Bri mumbled beside me. "They said that window was sealed shut."

"Oh," I said.

A faint glow came through the window. I was able to see that we were in a small, damp cellar. Beneath my bare feet was a cold, gritty concrete floor scattered with old straw. Behind me, I saw that Marcus was still knocked out. I stepped toward the window but made it only a few feet before my stomach churned, and I plopped myself on a damp mattress.

Marcus groaned. Bri sat next to me.

"Hey," I said as I shook Marcus.

Then the door rattled. Bri and I froze. The door flew open, and a short, broad-shouldered man with a patchy beard stood in front of me. He appeared younger than the hipster I'd seen just before being knocked on the head. I wondered if this was the man who had hit me.

"Well, come along," said the stranger in a weary tone.

"Not on your life," I said, tightening my fists. Bri held on to me.

As the man stepped forward, a sudden flash and snap of electricity surged in his hand. I backed away.

"We could, you know, use this if you like that sort of thing," the man said firmly, as though he was tired of repeating himself.

"I don't like that kind of stuff, sicko," I said. "And I'm not coming with you."

A taller, lankier man with a patchy beard rushed in and grabbed me. I screamed, kicked, and punched, but he wasn't fazed one bit. I continued to fight against him as he dragged me. Then, the broad-shouldered man with the Taser slammed the door shut as the lanky man continued to drag me into a dimly lit hallway of a narrow cellar with makeshift walls and doors. None of the doors we passed looked like they belonged there; they were framed with thin plywood and walled with unpainted, aging sheetrock. I pulled away from the man dragging me but stopped when I heard another zap behind me.

"Up we go," the lanky man said with glee. "You'll like this."

I doubt that, I thought. If these men were doing this to me, what horror had they already done to Bri? She and I had barely had time to talk, but I could tell she wouldn't be the same.

"Where are you taking me?" I asked. "What are you planning?"

There was pounding on the door behind us, and I could hear a muffled voice.

"Let her go!" Marcus yelled from behind the door. "Somebody, help us!"

"Now, now," said the lanky man dragging me. "Looks like your friend wants to get out." The man stopped moving. "But we don't need him, do we?" He turned toward me and grinned. Aside from his patchy beard, his nose was red and puffy, like he'd been in several fights and had lost each one.

"You're getting a good look at me, I see," the lanky man said. With a grin, he added, "That's...good."

It is good, so I can better identify you later in a lineup, I thought. I glared at him. I needed to get back to Marcus before they did something terrible to us.

"All right," the lanky man said, turning away and dragging me again. "Move it!"

"You still need to tell me where you're taking me," I demanded. I flinched when I heard another zap behind me. "Okay, I hear you loud and clear. Can you at least tell me where my shoes are?"

"It's best not to ask questions." As he spoke, he didn't even look at me. "Just...enjoy the ride."

"Ewww, I don't think so." I struggled against his grip. Despite all appearances, he was surprisingly strong.

"What's wrong?" he asked, his eyes widening as if this was a shocking revelation. Then he turned toward me. "You don't—"

His next words were cut off as he groaned and dropped to the floor.

I had kicked the guy in the balls and then ran like hell. The man with the Taser shouted as he began his pursuit.

I wished I knew where I was going. The hallway didn't provide any clues, and I didn't even know if I was still in the cottage. The cellar floor was made of deteriorating concrete that tore into my bare feet, but I ignored the pain.

When I came to some steps, I took them two at

a time. The broad-shouldered man was right behind me. I determined at that moment that I needed to get that Taser from him. Just before I reached the top, I glanced behind me and slammed into someone. I was propelled backward, and I would have fallen down the steps, possibly to my death, if I hadn't been caught by the broad-shouldered man's rough hands. I felt his Taser dig into my side as he pulled me into the wet, musty flannel he wore.

He pushed me forward, and I came face-to-face with the hipster: beard, cold blue eyes, and man bun. The hipster held my shoulders with both hands.

"Alissa," he said softly. "You're going to hurt yourself running around like this."

"You're...the guy...who..." I stammered.

"Who what?" he asked innocently as he gripped my arms. "I'm just the guy, and you're just the girl we need right now. As a matter of fact, my colleague, who you apparently assaulted, should be joining us soon." He smiled. "He and his brother have something special planned for you." A clomping from down below caught my ears.

"Gross," I spat. "Just kill me now."

"Oh, I wouldn't do that," the lanky man wheezed. He was still hunched over, holding himself. He smirked and turned toward the broad-shouldered man. Seeing them side by side like that, I could make out the family resemblance. The lanky man turned and went down the steps. Then, he turned back toward me and licked his dry, chapped lips. "I've been thinking that I know a few guys who'd like to meet you. You can thank the boss for that." The lanky man gestured to the hipster, who remained at the top of the steps. "He wanted to kill you and your two friends outright. But I know some locals who...you know."

The lanky man brushed by me, inhaling my scent, and caressed my arm. I shivered and felt dirty.

"What do you mean?" I asked shakily. I hated myself for not being able to keep my voice together. "And what's with your nose?"

The boss laughed, and his cold blue eyes danced. "Joey couldn't stay away from you kids, so I taught him a lesson."

Joey—the lanky man—flinched. "You promised you wouldn't use our names."

"And you promised you'd go nowhere near the camp," the boss said.

Joey shrank back. Now, I realized he was probably the same man Bri had encountered in the woods.

"Paul and Joey," the boss said. "Take this girl to the other room. We've got things to discuss with her."

Joey yanked me along. Behind me, Paul, his broad-shouldered brother, held the Taser. I gritted my teeth. Whatever these three guys had planned wasn't going to go well for me. Still, I was determined to be tough, no matter what.

Chapter 19

Alissa

My entire body went rigid and my mind scrambled as I was tased once again. Seconds that felt like hours passed, and the device was removed.

Though I'd been ready for it this time, I still gasped, "Holy crap!" I'd never once imagined what tasing would feel like. Now I never would have to. I glared at my torturers. Joey was laughing but Paul looked on somberly. I could tell he didn't want to be doing this. Though he looked like a real bruiser, there was definitely a teddy-bear quality to him. Their boss, still cool and collected, simply stood there, arms crossed and gazing at me with his cold blue eyes.

"What do"—I gasped, still feeling the shock of electricity coursing through me—"you guys want?"

No one seemed interested in responding to my question, which pissed me off. They'd already asked me numerous vague questions that ranged from What do you know about us? To Why are you here?

I added, trying to put a little cool in my voice, "Like I said before. We're just trying to get his little sister." I avoided using Marcus' and Bri's names.

Paul loaded another cartridge in the stun gun and took aim. I felt myself tense up. I didn't know how much of this a person could take. Another jolt terrified me. The boss placed his hand on Paul's arm. He spoke calmly. "That's enough. I believe her. We've already done this to her three times with the same result. Don't need to kill her right now."

Paul seemed to slump at this statement as he approached me.

I heard the boss, but I wanted his remark to mean something else. "So, you're letting us all go, then?" I asked.

The boss chuckled at this statement but didn't

answer me. I decided I'd pay this guy back if I ever got free. He stepped out of the room, saying, "You know what to do."

I struggled against Paul as he pulled me up.

His brother, Joey, cackled and licked his lips. "You're a feisty one, aren't you?"

I spat at him. "Wouldn't you like to know."

"Easy there, sweetheart," Paul whispered in my ear, as if he were soothing a horse. "I'm just going to untie your feet so you can walk a little."

I stood still, glaring at Joey. As Paul knelt down, I'd already planned my next move. When he finished untying my feet, I reared back and kicked him right in the face.

Paul tumbled back, grabbing at his face. Joey, caught off guard, hesitated. I didn't give him any time to get with the program. I turned and ran. As well as I could, anyway. My muscles still seemed to be experiencing a little shock. Joey tried to cut me off as I headed toward the only door. I smacked him in his sore nose, and some of his blood splattered right in my face as he howled in pain. Me, I darted through the door and smacked right into the boss.

"Going somewhere?" he asked.

I looked up. Though my insides seemed to rev like a well-oiled engine, I couldn't move. The boss' cool blue eyes communicated a surprisingly calm demeanor, like he knew this was going to happen and he was just waiting for me right by the door.

The click of a gun cocking behind me caused me to tense up even more.

"Let's kill her now!" Joey cackled. "I wanted to do other things to her first, but—"

"Please," I said, feeling tears forming in my eyes. "I'm just a kid. I promise I won't—"

The boss interrupted me by holding up his hand. "We won't kill you since, after all, you're just a kid. But something else might."

"What?" I shouted, desperate to know more. Between the tears and the shouting, I knew I sounded weak and terrified. I hated myself for it, but I had to get out of here, and I had to make sure Marcus and Bri would get out of here, too. "What about my friends?"

The boss shrugged. "You be good now. Paul," he said, addressing the shorter man, "you make sure she's locked up tight with the other two."

"Why are you using our names?" Paul said with a grimace.

The boss shrugged. "Because you're a local."

"I could use yours," Paul threatened.

"And you'd be dead."

I looked from Paul to his brother Joey, to this boss of theirs. I thought Paul, being wider and huskier than this bearded man, could probably take him in a fight. But he'd need some convincing. A plan for a diversion was already forming in my head. I just needed time to let it develop while these three, and whoever else was with them, figured out what they'd be doing.

"C'mon, Paul," I said, trying to match the boss' cool, calm voice. "Let's go back to my room. I'm tired and hungry anyway. Do you have anything to eat?"

Confusion passed over Paul's face. His mouth opened, then closed, then opened again. Paul inhaled a deep breath and exhaled. I let him pull me away from the others, from the chair, and from the restraints.

He led me down a short hallway. As we passed an open doorway, I caught a glance inside. There was a table and what looked like a chemistry set inside.

"So," I perked up like I was starting a casual conversation. "What're you guys up to?"

Paul continued to pull me along in silence.

I tried again, trying to sound pleasant. "I mean, you heard the guy. You'd be dead anyway. Clearly, you're not camping out. You're working on something. Maybe you're kidnapping kids and selling them to the highest bidder. Maybe you're—"

Suddenly, Paul yanked me toward him and grabbed both of my shoulders tightly. I felt tears sting the corners of my eyes. "Look, little girl," he said through gritted teeth. "You weren't part of the plan. If the younger one hadn't seen my brother..." Paul's voice trailed off. "It doesn't matter. You three are all expendable." Paul paused and when he continued, his voice wavered. "Because you're some of Uncle Tom's kids, I'm trying to keep you alive. You understand me?"

His grip tightened on my shoulders. I bit my bottom lip and tasted blood. I inhaled and stared him straight in the eyes. "Who's Uncle Tom?"

Paul loosened his grip but didn't let go. His face softened as he spoke. "I went to Camp Lenape. Same as you. Uncle Tom was my camp counselor. You know, Tom Roberts?"

I opened my mouth, but I was too stunned to say anything. Marcus and Nate had told me that Mr. Roberts was somehow in on all this. I just didn't know how, or what these guys were doing at this old cottage.

An engine revved from somewhere near the front of the cottage. Paul froze and listened. I was about to say something snarky, but the front door creak open. Paul ushered me quickly down the steps. He didn't even stop to help me up when I lost my footing on one of the steps. We came to what I took to be the room I'd shared with Marcus. Paul stopped at the door.

"I sincerely hope you and your friends will be okay," he said.

With crossed arms and a sneer, I said, "Whatever."

He frowned and pulled the door open. I stepped inside. The door slammed shut, dooming us all if we couldn't get out of there soon.

Chapter 20

Marcus

"Well, what're we going to do?" asked Bri. She stood there with her hands on her hips.

We'd exhausted all possibilities of escape. In fact, Bri had led me through every corner and crevice of the room to confirm there was no way out. Now, it was my turn to stand with my hands on my hips. My little sister hated it when I copied her, so she changed her posture. I stared at the door, wondering how Nate would get out of the room if he were here.

"Wait!" I held my breath as I dug in my front

pocket and pulled out the multitool Nate had given me. I held it high, as though I were wielding Excalibur.

"What're you going to do with that?" Bri asked. "Cut us out?"

"Actually," I said, examining the pins in the door hinges, "if you crouch down and pull the door up, I could push the pins up and out the hinges."

"Okay," Bri said with defeat in her voice. I understood. She'd already been here for at least twenty-four hours.

She placed her fingers beneath the door and pulled up. As I began to work the first hinge with the multitool's screwdriver, I made a mental note to thank Nate for his foresight. A pin shifted, but I stopped pushing when I heard voices approaching.

"I sincerely hope you and your friends will be okay," a man's voice came from the other side of the door.

"Whatever," came Alissa's voice. I didn't need to see her to know that her arms were crossed, and her hips were jauntily placed as she addressed the man.

The lock turned, and Bri and I stepped away from the door. I crouched low and prepared to tackle whoever came through.

With a downcast face, Alissa stepped into the

room. A stocky man behind her slammed the door shut.

"Alissa, are you okay?" I asked. I reached to embrace her, but she pulled back.

"No, I'm not," she whispered. She sat down.

"What happened?" I sat down next to her and fiddled with the multitool. Bri sat on her other side and wrapped an arm around her.

"I was tased, for one thing," Alissa said. There was a steeliness in her voice, even though it was clear she'd been shaken up. Alissa went on. "We're dead if we don't get out of here."

Gripping the multitool, I stood and began to pace.

"This guy Paul told me he was a camper at Camp Lenape," Alissa continued. "I think he wants to help us, but his boss with the man bun is hell-bent on killing us."

"Are you sure?" I asked. "You don't think—"

"Oh, I don't think," Alissa interjected. "I know." She shot me a don't-question-me look, so I shut my big mouth.

"Anyway," Alissa continued. "They didn't tell me what they were up to. But there's a makeshift lab in one of the rooms. Marcus, we've got to get out of here now. I think they plan to set this place on fire with us locked inside."

"I won't let that happen," I said confidently. "That's why I brought this." I held up the multitool.

Alissa's voice perked up. "Just let us know what you need."

I figured the pins in the door hinges needed some more pressure to make them slide easier. Alissa and Bri bent down and slid their fingers between the base of the door and the floor to pull it up. I tried the pin again.

"It's moving!"

"That's great," Alissa grunted. "Can you get it to move any faster? I think someone's coming."

"Get up," I said. "Let's get behind the door."

Alissa and Bri rose. I motioned for Bri to step into the center of the room as a diversion. Alissa and I stepped back. We stood against the wall, so we'd be right behind the door when it swung open. The doorknob wiggled.

I was behind Alissa and tapped her shoulder. She looked at me. I mouthed, When the door opens, we push fast and hard.

"I have no idea what you said," she whispered. "But we should hit whoever this guy is with the door. Give me your multitool."

"Okay," I whispered back and handed her the multitool, which she quickly closed and reopened. I was glad that she was thinking the same thing as me.

The door opened. We shoved it back. The door thudded and bounced on someone's boot.

"Nice try, kids," a man's voice said. "Really nice try. But..." His voice trailed off, and then there was a zap that sounded like a Taser. "We need the boy now. Marcus, I believe that's his name. You can come willingly or by force." He zapped the Taser again. "Trust me. We want this to go as smooth as possible."

There was no time to plan, but I knew neither of us could go with this creep. Alissa raised the knife from the multitool high. In one motion, she stepped around the door and stabbed at the man as he took a step forward.

The man cursed. The Taser he held clattered to the floor as he grabbed, with even more cursing, at his shoulder.

Alissa grabbed the door and slammed it three times. The third time, I added more force to the slam. The center of the door cracked, and the man dropped to the floor. She knelt beside him and picked up the Taser, then began rummaging through his pockets.

"Hey, Paul, are you okay down there?" called a man from upstairs.

"Follow me," Alissa said as she rose. "Bri, don't look at the man on the floor." She stuffed the Taser and a few other items in her pocket. Turning left out of the door, she stepped over the man groaning on the floor. I covered Bri's eyes and guided her in front of me and out the door.

Then, heavy footsteps descended the stairs.

The hallway we were in grew darker until the only thing I could make out was Alissa's bright orange T-shirt. She turned a corner.

"Marcus, put your hand up slowly," she instructed.

I did as I was told and hit a damp two-by-four. I crouched.

"I'm not sure where we are," Alissa whispered. "But I think we're in some kind of cubby."

We continued to move deeper into the cubby, which was more like a narrow, low hallway. I kept scraping my shoulders on the walls.

"Oh, kids," a man said playfully, as if we were in the middle of a game of hide-and-go-seek, which we sort of were, but not really. "I know you're in here. There's no escape." He paused. "What the hell! You stabbed my brother in the shoulder!"

Just then, I heard a creaky noise above, and the dawning light crept over us.

Chapter 21

Alissa

I wished I could take credit for opening the cellar doors above us, but I couldn't. Marcus and Bri both gasped. I was just as surprised as they were when the doors began to creak, and a sliver of light shone on us. We stood with gaping mouths as we squinted in the sudden brightness of the morning sun.

"Get a move on!" yelled Joey, making me jump. He'd caught up to us. "We're leaving."

"We're going for a ride," said a familiar voice.

We looked up to see the boss' close-cropped

beard. His eyes seemed colder and bluer than when I last saw him.

"Nice man bun, dude," Marcus said flatly.

"Marcus, that's enough," said the boss. "Let's go. All of you."

We were still barefoot and standing chest-deep on the steps that led upward and out of the cellar. We were also chest-deep in a heap of trouble if we didn't devise a plan.

"You heard the man," Joey said. "Let's go. I'll keep watch from here." He chuckled.

I know he's watching my behind, I thought. I wanted to kick Joey, but I knew that wouldn't be wise. I glanced at Marcus, searching his face for an inkling of a plan. It wasn't there. I nodded a tight smile toward Bri, hoping to reassure her that everything would be okay. I had the Taser safely tucked in my shorts. In less than a couple of steps, one of us would be in the clutches of the boss, while the other would be with Joey. I would most likely end up with Joey, and I couldn't let that happen.

I took a step up. Marcus and Bri did the same. Joey followed. I didn't get the sense that he had a weapon as he reached to push me along. Before he could touch me, I turned on him. I grabbed the Taser out of my shorts and hit him with a charge right in the face. He was down instantly, while Marcus plowed the boss right in the gut. I gave the boss a zap for good measure before I motioned to Bri to follow Marcus.

As we ran down the gravel driveway and came to the road, we heard sirens and stopped.

"Should we just wait, then?" Marcus asked.

"You want us to stop right in the pathway of a cop car?" I asked with a grin.

"Very funny," Marcus said dryly. "I mean, we have to be in sight, especially since these guys are going to recover and be after us again."

"How do we know they're coming for us?"

Marcus shrugged. "We don't, but we need to get their attention."

Trying to ignore the loose gravel digging into our bare feet, the three of us waited on either side of the driveway to allow room for a car to pull in. In a moment, we would be safe. Joey and the boss would be arrested, and Paul would be treated and arrested.

A cruiser with flashing lights pulled up to us. We didn't even have to wave it down. The officer in the driver's seat rolled down the window. His partner looked at us from the front passenger's seat. A breath caught in my throat as I recognized the men as Officer Duvall and Officer Rogers. I stepped back.

"Hey, kids," Officer Rogers began. "You must be Alissa Claude and Marcus Kahale." He looked down at Bri. "And you, little lady, must be Bri

Kahale."

Marcus and Bri nodded eagerly. I stiffened. I didn't trust these officers. Not after the way they'd shown up out of nowhere at the call box. Their appearance now, plus the way they knew our names, gave me even more reason not to trust them. Officer Duvall, the driver, opened his door and stepped out.

"Great," Officer Duvall said. "Your friends Janice Kane and Nate Wilson reported you missing."

"When did you see them?" I asked.

"They came to the station," Officer Duvall said with a smile.

Officer Rogers followed close behind his partner as both men approached us, each with a hand on the gun at his hip.

"When?" I asked, backing away warily. Seeing Marcus and Bri tense up, I knew they'd also picked up on the officers' aggressive approach.

"Maybe about an hour and a half ago," Officer Duvall said. "They were great kids and worried about you."

"If that's the case, why do I feel like we're being apprehended, like criminals?" Marcus asked. He inched near me. "Run, you two!"

I had already felt the urge to run, but I wasn't fast enough. One of the officers tased me, and I fought against the paralyzing pain. Falling to the ground in disbelief at being zapped for a fourth time, I struggled to keep my eyes open.

"I got her!" Duvall shouted. "Did you get the boy and the little girl?"

"Nah," Rogers said. "We'll send someone back into the woods later to get them. They won't get very far."

Somehow, the pain became more bearable as I rose to my knees, thankful that Marcus and Bri got away.

Duvall laughed as he knelt over me and cuffed my hands in front of me. He pulled me up. "You take her to the car," he told Rogers, "and I'll go check on the guys in the cottage."

Duvall passed me off to Rogers, who dragged me. I stumbled as I tried to regain full use of my legs. Rogers stuffed me in the back of the squad car.

"Hey!" I screamed. "Watch it! You goon!"

Rogers pulled me close. "You watch it!"

We both froze when we heard two sharp gunshots. Panic rose in my chest. I tried to fight back tears, but a flood was already coming. Rogers yanked the seatbelt over me and buckled it.

Another gunshot went off. Rogers' face was stony as he got behind the wheel and slammed the car door. If I got out of here, I planned on getting this officer so good, he wouldn't even be able to recognize himself in the mirror.

"I took care of that prick with the goofy man bun on his head," said Duvall. He carried a duffel bag on his shoulder. "I handled Joey, too."

"What about the boy and the other girl?" Rogers asked. "We can't leave any loose ends."

"You let them get away," said Duvall as he shrugged and walked toward the car door. "It happens."

Bittersweet relief flooded over me. Officer Duvall, if you could call him an officer, hadn't shot Marcus and Bri. He'd shot Joey and his boss. Still, I felt sick to my stomach.

As the car pulled away, I shifted so I could catch a glimpse of the time. It was already well past six in the morning. It had been hours since we parted ways with Nate and Janice. They must've found help by now. I stared out the window. Hot tears began to form in my eyes. But they weren't tears of sadness or fear; they were tears of anger. We'd gotten to this point to save Bri. Now, I was the one who needed saving.

Chapter 22

Marcus

Bri and I were lying hidden beneath some brush. I still couldn't believe what I'd seen. This officer had shot two unarmed men, wiped the gun clean, placed it in the hand of one of the men, and fired again. He'd then walked right into the cottage and exited with a duffel bag.

I looked at Bri. "You okay?"

"No," she replied, shaking her head. "Let's get out of here."

"Stay here a minute."

I took care to watch my footing as I descended

the bank. I didn't want Bri anywhere near the dead bodies. I didn't want her anywhere near me, either, in case I got caught. A car door slammed, and the patrol vehicle started up. I raced to the clearing to see it hang a left out the driveway. I caught the vehicle's ID: 572.

I went to the basement entrance, a future crime scene with two dead men. I knelt by the first one. He was young, maybe nineteen. I cringed as I felt his pockets. There was a bulge in one in the shape of a phone. As I reached inside the pocket, someone grabbed my ankle. I screamed. The bearded man behind me gurgled.

"Help me," he rasped. "Don't...leave me."

I kicked his hand away and pulled the cell phone out of the pocket of the younger man, who was clearly dead.

"Please," the bearded man said. "I beg you."

I stood and took a step back, bumping into someone behind me. When I turned around, Bri was there.

"Marcus, is he..." she paused. Her eyes grew wide.

"I told you to stay undercover!" I shouted.

Tears began to well up in her eyes. "I know. I just..."

"I'm sorry," I said, hugging her close. "I'm a little jumpy. We both are."

She nodded into my shoulder. "We need to help

Alissa and that man right there."

"You're right."

The phone I took from the young guy was a flip phone. I hadn't seen one since I was seven, when my dad gave me his to play with when he first upgraded to a smartphone. I checked the screen.

"No signal," I said to Bri as I held the phone open. I glanced at the cottage, wishing for my own smartphone. Maybe it would do better, but there wasn't time to waste. I snapped the phone shut and turned to Bri. "We need to get out of these woods and find a better signal."

Bri nodded. "We need to stay off the roads, too. Just in case those guys are looking for us."

We headed toward the road. To the right, the road sloped upward. We entered the woods but made sure to stay within the cover of the trees.

We walked about a mile before I rechecked the signal. There was one bar. One single hope that I'd be able to reach help. I dialed 9-1-1. A single ring was followed by a steady beep, then silence. In the distance, I heard sirens.

"Did you get through?" Bri asked. "Are they coming to help us?"

"I don't know," I said. "Phone's not working."

I wondered where we were and where the call box was that Alissa had mentioned. I began to move again and raised the cell phone again. Like us, its signal was lost. Bri, I could tell, was exhausted—and I couldn't even begin to imagine what Alissa was going through.

Chapter 23

Alissa

"You guys could probably slow down!" I shouted at the two officers in front of me. I'd been yelling at them for some time. Finally, the younger one, Rogers, who was driving, told me to shut up. I didn't.

"What are your plans, anyway?" I questioned them. "Let me guess. Dump the body and head north into Canada? If you do that, can you make sure that I at least have a nice view of a lake? I read Walden Pond last school year, and I just love the idea of fading off into tranquility."

"You sure can talk," said Rogers with a snort. "I bet the boys love a chatterbox like you."

At that remark, I kicked the back of Rogers' seat, which made him bounce forward. He glared at me in the rearview mirror.

"Take care of her, will you," Rogers snapped at Duvall.

Duvall turned.

"Stop it," he demanded. "Or I will—"

"Did you say, 'You will'?" I asked, feigning surprise. "I'm so glad because I was worried you wouldn't."

Really, I was not at all like this. Under normal circumstances, even normal high-stress conditions, I would generally keep my cool. But I guess being zapped four times with the threat of being killed caused me to act out of character.

"Hey," I said. "You want to hear a joke?"

They didn't answer.

"Fine," I said. "Since you don't object, here we go. There once was a man, who taught some kids about personal character, but here's the punchline. He had none of his own! I'm sure you two know who I'm talking about, right?"

No response. I sulked. I still couldn't believe Mr. Roberts was involved in all this mess. Just a couple nights ago, he'd had us watching skits about personal character.

I sighed. "I guess the irony is lost on you both."

Rogers took his eyes off the road to look at me. "Listen, kid. If you—"

"Look out!" I shouted.

A dark SUV was barreling down the road. Duvall grabbed the steering wheel and spun it to the right. The police cruiser veered off the road. I bounced up and down against the hard leather. My seatbelt dug into my chest and neck. Pine branches slapped against the side of the vehicle, but Rogers managed to avoid hitting a single tree. That is, until we plowed into a downed log. The airbags in the front exploded with a puff. I gasped as the seatbelt tugged at my waist and chest before pulling me back against the seat.

The three of us groaned with various levels of pain. I unhooked my seatbelt and reached for the door. As I opened it, the vehicle was swarmed by a horde of police officers. Their guns were trained on Rogers and Duvall, who were still face-first in inflated nylon.

A woman helped me open the door as she identified herself, but I could focus only on the black-and-white logo of the agency embroidered on her vest: DEA.

As I rose, I couldn't help but wonder what Mr. Roberts had gotten us into. For the moment, I didn't really care. I needed my parents. I needed to know Bri and Marcus were okay.

Marcus.

I thought about the way he gazed at me with his hazel eyes. My heart skipped a beat. Then, the thought passed. There'd be plenty of time for that later. For now, I needed to get the hell away from this camp.

Chapter 24

Marcus

Sirens ceased, and a dark SUV pulled to the side of the road just as I stepped out to check the signal once more. I tensed and glanced back to the line of trees to see if Bri was visible. She wasn't. I turned.

The rear passenger door opened, and Nate climbed out.

"Marcus!" he shouted.

"Nate, what're you doing here?" I asked.

"Dude, this is crazy!" he said. Behind him, Janice hopped out of the SUV.

"Hey, Bri!" Janice ran past me. I turned around, and she was giving Bri a big hug.

Another vehicle, like the first, pulled up. A man and a woman dressed in dark uniforms got out. When they got close, I saw that their vests identified them as DEA agents.

"What's this all about?" I asked. "Where's Alissa? She was with me at the cottage. Then some dirty cops picked her up in squad car five seventy-two. Is she okay? Did they find the car?"

"Bro," Nate said, putting his hands on my shoulders. "Calm down. Breathe slowly."

My gaze darted from agent to agent, then back to Nate. I couldn't believe he could be so relaxed at a time like this.

"She's all right," Nate said. "Her captors were picked up after they crashed, but she's okay. They're taking her back to the camp. Our parents are already there. Let's get in the car, okay?"

I nodded, letting Nate lead me to the backseat of the SUV. He even reached over and buckled me in like I was some little kid. Janice and Bri got into the other SUV.

As we drove, Nate gave me the details.

"After you guys got caught, we ran into town," he explained. "We had a hell of a time trying to get help. The police were stonewalling us until Uncle Craig showed up. He said something suspicious was going on at the camp. Kids were missing. Mr.

Roberts was gone, and so was Aunt Lauren. That's when I told the police about the financials we saw at the cottage. They told us to wait. It was hours before someone showed up, even though the DEA had already been watching the place."

My eyes bulged. I was speechless—I had no idea how deep the crime ran at Camp Lenape. Nate was more into spy stuff than me, so I let him continue to talk about the DEA sting. I was just glad Bri was safe. And a big part of me desperately wanted to see Alissa.

I was tired of being the wallflower at every single dance, and tonight's luau would clearly be canceled. I'd been planning to ask Alissa to this year's dance, but there'd be plenty of opportunities to ask her out, and I wouldn't waste the first chance I got. This morning could've been it for us, and I wouldn't ever have been able to tell her that I'd been in love with her for years.

Epilogue

Wednesday, August 15.

Light smoke billowed from several grills. The smell of barbecue chicken, hot dogs, and hamburgers wafted through the air. Middle school boys and girls kicked balls across soccer fields. Others played a pickup game of basketball or cornhole or just lounged around. The kids shied away from the adults, as parents, teachers, and administrators looked on.

Marcus and Alissa held hands as Bri ran ahead to catch up with friends from her elementary school and meet new classmates for the first time. Marcus smiled. Alissa wrapped an arm around him as they followed. Today was a welcome picnic to Bri's new middle school. He and Alissa had finished their eighth-grade year here three years ago, which seemed like a distant memory compared to their more vivid, harrowing experience at Camp Lenape.

When they'd been found and reunited with their parents, the campground was already swarming with parents helping their kids pack for home. Several parents were swearing they'd be suing the camp for putting their kids in danger. But Marcus had doubted they would get much, if anything, for their efforts.

Mr. Roberts, his wife, and his daughter, Aunt Lauren, had been arrested, though at the time Marcus didn't know why. Later, he found out that Mr. Roberts had somehow gotten involved with some guys from Detroit who were using the old cottage as a meth lab. Mr. Roberts had managed to receive enough money from the deal to keep the camp afloat for almost a summer.

Sort of.

The camp was already doomed. The Roberts family hadn't thought about the danger of their actions or realized the impact it would have on the campers, like Alissa and Bri. Alissa had woken up first, so the boss, Erik Novak, had decided to question her. Marcus had been knocked out. Bri had seen one of the meth-lab crew members. The crew didn't want to risk being exposed by a little kid, so they'd planned to hold her captive and unharmed until they cleared out. Their plans had become far more sinister when Marcus and Alissa barged in on them.

In the end, their plans had fallen apart. Joey had been killed by Officer Richard Duvall, who along with his crooked partner, Neil Rogers, had been providing protection to the meth lab. Both officers had been kicked off the force in disgrace and thrown in jail. Novak had barely survived, and he and Paul, who had recovered from the stab wound, would also be going to jail for a long time.

Marcus pulled Alissa closer as they walked.

"I'm glad we found Bri when we did," Marcus said quietly.

"I'm glad we got out when we did," said Alissa. She tightened her lips.

"Me, too." His gaze fell upon Bri, who had joined a few of her friends from elementary school. They seemed happy to see each other.

"Hey." Alissa squeezed him. "She'll be all right. You'll see."

"I know." Marcus nodded. "Therapy seems to be helping her. How about you?"

Alissa curled the side of her lip. "It's therapy," she said dryly. "What about you?"

"Same," he said.

They walked in silence, not daring to broach the subject of therapy again. Marcus hoped therapy wouldn't define their relationship, though he knew their shared experience, and the one Alissa had endured by herself, would always be part of who they were. They approached the games and stopped.

"You want to play some cornhole?" Marcus asked.

Alissa laughed. "Sure, bet I'll win."

Marcus picked up some beanbags and handed them to her. "If you do, I'll buy you a hot dog."

Alissa pushed him lightly. "The hot dogs are free. Now get over there and prepare to be beaten."

Marcus took the other side and watched as Alissa eyed the hole in the board next to him. Even though he'd known her for years, Marcus still couldn't get over how pretty she was. Her deep brown skin seemed to glow in the sun. When she stood upright, he liked the way she brushed a stray lock back over her ear. He also liked the way she flashed him a smile and took aim. She tossed a beanbag, which hit him right in the stomach.

"Ow," Marcus said, not liking that very much. "What was that for?"

Alissa grinned. "I think you know exactly what that was for."

"Well," Marcus said. "You'll be down a bag."

"I'll still beat you," Alissa smirked and waved. "Hey, guys!"

Marcus turned to see Janice and Nate jogging toward them. Nate slowed and stuffed a hot dog into his mouth. Janice sipped a cold coffee drink she'd gotten from the shop across the street.

"Oh my God," she groaned. "Have you guys heard? They're cutting the arts budget at school. Do you know what that means?"

Marcus stared at her blankly as Alissa chewed the inside of her lip and shook her head. Neither of them had been keeping up on the happenings at school.

"They're also cutting the sports budget," mumbled Nate between bites. "Some of the teachers are getting laid off, too."

"Again!" Marcus huffed. "How could they possibly do that every year and get away with it?"

"I don't know," Alissa said. "Maybe someone's stealing money."

Marcus, Nate, and Janice looked at her, mouths agape, waiting for an explanation.

Alissa shrugged. "I'm just saying."

Janice tapped Alissa's shoulder lightly. "Do you guys know what this means?"

"No," Marcus said, speaking for himself and Alissa.

Like a well-rehearsed segue, Nate answered. "It means we've got another mystery to solve." He pulled a rolled-up notebook out of his back pocket. "I even started a case log. We just need a name for our company. I was thinking—"

"What's this company thing?" Alissa asked, directing her question to Marcus.

"Oh, it's nothing," Marcus said. His face flushed. Alissa knew he and Nate snuck out at night every summer. But she didn't know about their childhood game of detective.

"C'mon," Alissa chided. "I want to know."

"Oh, look," said Marcus, changing the subject. "Bri's found the hot dog line. I'll get you one." He dropped the beanbags he'd been holding, took Alissa's hand, and grinned. "My treat."

Alissa laughed. "You're such a dork." As they walked, she bumped her hip against Marcus' side. "You will tell me about this company thing."

"It's kids' stuff," Marcus said. "But if you want to know..."

His voice trailed off as he and Alissa walked hand in hand. He couldn't help but overhear Nate and Janice, chatting excitedly about plans for sneaking into the principal's office. Maybe they'd find the rumored Jacuzzi installed last year. Or perhaps they'd see Principal Moss drive up in a brand-new Lamborghini that he'd bought with money pilfered from school funds. It was silly, but he had to admit that the idea of sneaking around and exposing corruption thrilled him.

Marcus looked at Alissa. Her eyes danced with amusement.

"You already know about our detective game," Marcus said.

"I do." Alissa wrapped her arm tighter around Marcus' waist. "But I want to hear it from you."

As he shared with Alissa how he and Nate had played detective in their many adventures at Camp Lenape, he realized how much his relationships would change and grow. Nate had always had his back. On many thrilling adventures, Nate had helped bring out the best of Marcus' honesty, courage, and good humor. That would never change. But Alissa did change things between Marcus and Nate. She'd had his back in the toughest of times. With her by his side, they could embark on even more adventures—perhaps as equal partners as they unraveled the many mysteries at Lenape High.

This thought thrilled him even more.

THE END

Acknowledgements

No creative work happens in a vacuum. Therefore, acknowledgement goes to those who critiqued this work in part and in whole throughout the writing process.

Robert Broomall, Keith Hoskins, Diane Foster, Amy Bock, Peggy Thompson, and Lisa Janele have adventured with me throughout the course of the year it took for me to flesh out and finalize this story. Without their honest criticism as beta readers and fellow writers, this work would have been a much different story than the one contained within the pages of this book."

Asha Fields at Field Day Press for her helping to bring this to a finalized draft through her professional beta readings, line editing, and teleconferencing.

Donna Ng for bringing this home through the final stages of proofreading.

Finally, thank you to those who have invested their time into reading this book. I do hope you enjoyed the read.

About the Author

Tim grew up in Syracuse, New York. He currently resides in Maryland where he teaches English, Creative Writing, Film, and Theatre on the middle school level. At the insistence of his own students, he began writing seriously in 2014.

He credits his love for story to his mother, who spent countless hours reading to him and his siblings when they were growing up. Growing up, he devoured the literary words of C. S. Lewis, J. R. R. Tolkien, Piers Anthony, and many others. Mysteries, thrillers, and fantasies are among the genre he most frequently reads.

When he's not writing, he's reading, teaching, camping, or enjoying a live music concert.

Visit Tim on the web at the following locations:
www.timothyrbaldwin.com
facebook.com/timothyrbaldwin
Twitter @timothyrbaldwin
Instagram @timothyrbaldwin

Made in the USA
Middletown, DE
13 July 2020